Children of the Euphrates

Layla Qurbānī

Translated by Blake Archer Williams
Illustrated by Leila Teymouri

LANTERN PUBLICATIONS

In the Name of God,
the Most Compassionate, the Most Merciful

Prayers of God's Peace and Blessings

In keeping with the Islamic practice of showing respect for the name of God, and sending prayers of God's peace and blessings whenever the name of His blessed Prophet, Lady Fātima, and the Twelve Imams is mentioned, as well as for asking God to hasten the reappearance of the Lord of the Age on the Earthly plane, one or more of the following Arabic symbols have been employed throughout the text. They are repeated for their great rewards.

 Used exclusively after the name of God, meaning "the Sublimely Exalted", or, as a prayer, "[May His name be] Sublimely Exalted".

 Used exclusively after the name of the Prophet, meaning "May the peace and blessings of God be unto him and unto [the purified and inerrant members of] his family"

 Used for any of the Twelve Imams or past prophets of God, meaning "May God's peace be unto him".

 Used for two or more of the Twelve Imams or past prophets of God, meaning "May God's peace be unto them".

 Used for Lady Fātima, meaning "May God's peace be unto her".

 Used for a plurality of the Fourteen Immaculates, meaning "May God's peace be unto them all collectively".

 Used for the Lord of the Age (the Twelfth Imam), meaning "May God hasten the advent of his noble person".

1

Sometimes things happen in life for which you have to let go of all your attachments, and free yourself of everything you value. Indeed, this is what our story is about.

It was night, and the village was steeped in a deep silence. The sound of stray dogs could be heard all around. The sky was full of twinkling stars. It was as if they were winking and were perhaps intent on gradually making the earth fall in love with them. Ali woke up in a freight. He had had a nightmare. Beads of sweat covered his whole face. He was breathing heavily. Mālik was calmly asleep next to him, and his eyes were closed comfortably; it was as if he was dreaming sweet dreams. He groped the ground with his hand, like someone whose eyes could not see anything, until his hand reached the earthenware jar. The jar felt cool against the warmth of his hand. He poured himself a bowl of water and drank it all in a single draft. He felt a little better now. He thought it would be better for him to go back to sleep so that he would not wake up the others. He lay down and kept his eyes closed with difficulty, but could he not sleep. When he opened his eyes, darkness was all he could see. He got up and cautiously made his way towards the door. He did his best to open the door quietly, but the wooden door creaked as it opened. It was lighter outside the room. He looked around. The courtyard was quiet, unlike during the day, when it was the playground of his little brothers and sisters. It was as if the ground and the walls and doors of the house were also resting before the start of their new day.

He felt weary. Although it is said that Arab boys become full-grown men while they are still in their teens, but they still have a heart. They will miss their loved ones. There are surely other things in one's life that one will be hard pressed to do without if one is deprived of them. He thought he had to make a decision; he either had to decide to leave, or he had to wipe all of last night's memories from his mind. This was the state of his mind when he realized he was leaning against the palm tree that was in the middle of the courtyard. He raised his head. The night sky was so beautiful. It had never seemed as beautiful to him, even when he and Mālik were in the desert and could not sleep and used to compete with each other to see who could count the most stars. They could never count them all.

Those memories might never be repeated for him, so he started counting. One, two, three...

As he was counting the stars, his eyes filled with tears. He lowered his head and wiped his tears away with his shirt sleeve. Men are not supposed to cry. This was a rite of passage: a necessary condition of becoming a man. He said to himself, who said that men don't cry? Surely every man who has said this has shed a tear or two at one time when they are alone and are feeling down. Why does being a man necessarily mean that he has to overcome his feelings? If Sa'd was there, he would surely have laughed at him from the bottom of his heart and joked about this for the rest of his life as his way of showing that he was more manly than Ali. In any event, this was one of the ways they competed with each other. He thought of what Mālik or Sa'd would do if they were in his place. He thought of the sheep and the white goat who had gotten loose of his tether and would go his own way every chance he got, leaving Ali behind to bear the brunt of his father's endless rebukes for not being a good shepherd. Mālik was better off; since his father had been martyred and his mother had passed away, Ali's father paid more attention to him in order to fill the void left by his father's absence.

Ali walked wearily towards the barn. He wanted to gaze at the white goat for hours through the hole in the wall. He must be yearning to get up to his usual mischief again. Next year, when Ali might not be around, the goat might give birth to a litter, and his mother would then milk the goat every morning.

He looked inside the barn. Not even a fly could be seen; it was covered in absolute darkness. He could only hear the sound of their breathing. Did sheep also have dreams? Did they miss each other when they were separated from each other? His mind was uneasy. When he turned his head, he saw Blacktail, their sheep dog, standing behind him, staring at him with wide-open eyes that looked like two white spheres under the starlight. Thank God; he had recognized Ali and had not woken up the whole village with those terrible barks of his which drove the wolves away and kept them at bay and at a great distance. Blacktail followed Ali's gaze and glanced up at the sky, gave out a faint whimper, and settled himself on the ground.

A hand was placed gently on Ali's shoulder, causing fear to rush through his whole being. He turned his head, his shoulder trembling with fear. It was Mālik. He was staring at Ali with his wavy hair, his mouth agape in a big yawn. Mālik said: "Don't even think about it; you'll either win or lose against Sa'd."

Ali regained his composure and spoke up.

"Why did you wake up?"

"Just pray that the Euphrates will be calm; the swim itself is nothing to be afraid of."

"What are you talking about? It's not as if it's the first time Sa'd's put on a swimming competition?"

Mālik laughed out loud and rubbed his sleepy eyes with his hands and said, "No, it is not the first time; but last time you lost to Sa'd. Try to make us proud this time around."

Ali envied Mālik's simplicity and kindheartedness. He was so loving. Although he was the referee, his eyes filled with tears, and he consoled Ali every time he lost to Sa'd. And now he was worried about Ali. God only knew what would happen if he knew what he was thinking. But what would ultimately come of it? Would he hide this great decision from them? No; that could not be. They were his closest friends. Either they would go along with him, or... or what?? Would they try to persuade him to change his mind, or prevent him from leaving? Mālik's voice brought Ali back from his thoughts. It seemed like he was tired and was going to go back to bed to sleep for the few hours that were left of the night.

"I'm going back to sleep. Come and sleep; everything will be over by tomorrow night."

Mālik's voice faded in the dark like Mālik himself. Ali leaned his head against the wall again and held his knees in his arms. His eyes refused to remain closed.

The rain had cast a handful of stars from the sky onto the blue surface of the river, and they sparkled among the bubbles made by the fish. Perhaps this was the earth's sky in which the stars shone during the day. A fishing line made of woven palm fronds was in the water, and Mālik was sitting on the ground by the river without blinking an eye. He wished he could catch an unlucky fish and grill it for his lunch. He sang to himself, and the thought never occurred to him that the croaking sound he made scared the fish away.

The sheep were grazing, each one busy eating away at a clump of grass. Their wool had a yellow tint to it. From a distance, it looked as if some large melons had been placed on the ground. Blacktail meandered around the herd and busied himself playing with a stray dog. But Ali was still distraught. His eyes were red from lack of sleep and his face reflected his weariness. He was crouched by the palm with his lute in his hand and was deep in thought. He was not paying any attention to the herd. There was a goat which was white all over, whose black eyes sparkled in the midst of his whiteness. He cast a look around, then slowly began to move away from the rest of the herd. It was the same white goat that had cut off the children's tether. When Ali was younger, one of the commanders of the Kūfan police who was passing through there on a mission had asked for the goat's mother because of its white wool and the goodness of its milk, and his father had presented the mother goat to him with both hands, as he was concerned about preventing anything untoward from happening. And now, every time an opportunity arose, the mother goat's kid would walk away from the herd in the direction where the police commander had taken his mother. Ali understood well that animals also have feelings and emotions, and that they missed each other. That's why he left the poor animal alone and never did anything like Mālik did, who yanked at the goat's hair each time he caught up with him.

The waves of the Euphrates gradually rose up and reached Mālik's feet. His legs were covered with mud and had muddied the whiteness of the long shirt that covered his legs. Suddenly his hand reached down, and his face broke out into a big smile, and he exclaimed loudly: "I got one! Ali! I got a fish!"

He got to his feet with difficulty and slowly and clumsily pulled at the line. He called Ali again and was overjoyed to see a luckless fish struggling at the end of his fishing line. But Ali did not hear him. Mālik jumped with joy, to the point that he almost lost his catch. He threw the fish onto the riverbank, and then threw his line back into the water, with greater force this time. The sound of his singing filled the whole plain. The life was going out of the fish as it struggled for water on the wet sands of the riverbank, desperately opening and closing its mouth.

Blacktail noticed someone approaching from a distance. He looked around the herd and went forward. When he could see more clearly, he wagged his tail as he recognized Sa'd, and made his way toward him, panting and grumbling. The white goat, who had been recaptured, bleated gloomily. The sheep of the herd baaed when they saw Sa'd and the white goat. They must have shared the stories of the white goat's escapes with their friends.

Ali was propped up against the palm tree while seated on the ground, and was journeying in his world of imagination, oblivious of Mālik's catch and the escape of his white goat. Sa'd called out to him several times and got annoyed and placed the goat on Ali's head. The white goat bleated loudly and wrapped its legs around Ali's head, then slipped down slowly to the ground, where he leapt out of Sa'd's reach. Ali was dumbfounded. In his confused stated, he said, "It's still early."

Sa'd was taken aback by Ali's words. He frowned and wiped the sweat from his face with the sleeve of his long white shirt, which was covered with dust. There was a tinge of annoyance in his voice "Where have you been? What kind of shepherd are you?"

He grabbed Ali by his collar and said, "If it wasn't for me, you would have been looking for your little goat until dusk! What do you think you're doing?!"

Upon seeing Sa'd, Mālik left the fish be and came closer, "I caught a fish." he said, "What are you talking about? Why have you grabbed Ali by his collar?"

Sa'd released Ali's collar agitatedly.

"I ran after him so much that I can't even stand up anymore!" Sa'd furiously exclaimed. "If I didn't feel sorry for you, I would roast the little rascal right now to teach its herd and ignorant shepherd a lesson."

Mālik chuckled but Ali did not say anything. He walked over to the goat, which was crouched in the crook of a palm tree, with its eyes fixed on the path he was brought back from and ignoring Ali. Ali picked him up and hugged him gently and caressed his face. His eyelids were wet. His big black eyes betrayed a heavy heart. He snuggled up to Ali's arms. Sa'd and Mālik looked at Ali in surprise.

Sa'd asked Mālik what had happened using eye and hand gestures, but Mālik, who was unaware of everything, shrugged and went back to his fishing. The waves had become larger and were hitting the shore more intensely, as if they wanted to take back their fish from Mālik. When Mālik saw the waves, he said loudly, "Sa'd, Ali can't swim today. The Euphrates has become dangerous."

Sa'd, who was annoyed by the behavior of the two of them, said "I will defeat the waves as well; this is Sa'd you are up against! If Ali is too scared to swim, then he will have forfeited the race."

Ali, who was still caressing the goat's face, turned slowly and looked at Sa'd, "Sa'd, you will miss me when I'm gone."

Sa'd smiled and stood next to Ali. One could never tell whether he was going to laugh or cry. He was unpredictable.

"I don't know whether or not I will miss you, but I do know one thing."

Ali's eyes were waiting for Sa'd to speak up and finish what he had to say.

"I am sure that if you continue the kind of shepherding that you do, your father will kill you after the herd perishes!"

Sa'd said this and laughed out loud, while it brought a frown to Ali's face. Mālik who had been amused by Sa'd's sardonic sense of humor, approached them with three fish whose innards he had gutted with a knife. He raised them up to show them and was as happy as he would be if he had won a great victory. "Look here, I caught all three myself, whereas all you two can do is argue."

He put the fish next to the palm tree. Blacktail rushed over to the fish, and Mālik, who wanted to go gather some firewood, chased him away roughly in order to teach Blacktail not to encroach on his food.

The fish were skewered and grilled. Mālik gave Ali and Sa'd their share, but not before spinning the skewers in his hands several times. Now each of them had a large skewer of deliciously grilled fish. Sa'd, who was giving Ali the evil eye, tasted some of his fish and placed his skewer on the fire again.

"Why do you look like a madman today? Has your father reprimanded you again about the herd?", asked Sa'd.

Mālik, who was staring at his grilled fish, answered, "No, his father didn't say anything. Ali just hasn't been able to get much sleep. It's a good job the

Euphrates is turbulent, because there is no saying what it would have done with Ali in the state that he is in."

"It will calm down if we give it a little time." Replied Sa'd.

Sa'd and Mālik continued to argue over the suitability of the Euphrates for a swimming race. Ali plunged a stick deeper into the fire, thinking of the words spoken last night by his father and his father's friends their words swirled around his mind.

Father: "I have made my decision. One of these nights, I will take the road to Kūfa and leave. I might come across his caravan."

Mālik: "They say the roads are unsafe. Ubaidullah's soldiers are everywhere."

Umar: "What of it? I heard that Hāni and Muslim were killed in Kūfa. I am sure that with the arrival of Husain ibn Ali ﷺ, Ibn Ziād will start a bloody war."

Ali's Father: "True. If we head out, there will be no coming back."

Suddenly, Mālik grabbed Ali's skewer, which was falling from his hand. The fish's head was burnt, but the body was ready to eat.

"You ruined the fish!" cried Mālik. "What were you thinking? I'm getting pretty sure that you have gone mad!"

"He is not feeling well" quipped Sa'd. "First he hugs and caresses a kid goat, and now he burnt his kebab."

Ali looked at the two of them. He snatched the skewer away from Mālik's hand, tore off a piece of the fish, and put it in his mouth.

"I want to go."

Mālik and Sa'd stared at Ali in disbelief.

"Didn't you hear what I said? I want to go with my father and his friends."

"Where to??" questioned Sa'd.

The fish had gotten stuck between Mālik's teeth. After a long span of time, he would resume eating the fish if he wasn't so concerned for Ali. He glanced over at Sa'd.

"What did they say last night?" asked Mālik.

Sa'd was now even more confused. His eyes were wandering back and forth between Ali and Mālik.

"Where are your father and his friends going?" asked Sa'd.

Suddenly his face darkened with worry. He threw what was left of his fish and its bones to Blacktail, who dared not come close for fear of Mālik. The poor animal wagged its tail, grabbed the fishbone, and made its way over to its friend. Sa'd asked in a hushed voice "Are they going to Kūfa? Don't they know that anyone who is seen around Kūfa or is seen exiting the city gets arrested by the police?"

"Do they really want to go? Like my father, who also went?" said Mālik.

"They want to go, and they know about the police. They even know that if they go, there is no coming back." said Ali.

Sa'd got up and gave out a laugh and patted the dust off his clothes, and then said, "And you want to go *with* them? I prefer to go where victory is to be had!"

"My father is going for the sake of Husain ibn Ali, the grandson of our Prophet!" replied Ali.

Mālik quickly ate up the rest of his fish. Blacktail was watching them closely. Ali threw the remnant of his fish toward him, and Blacktail caught it in the air.

"So then when are they leaving?" asked Sa'd.

"Some night soon." replied Ali.

"Will they take you with them? It is clear that Uncle will not give you his permission to leave," said Mālik.

"Of course he won't. I want to follow them once they have left the village so they can lead me to Husain ibn Ali's caravan."

"Have you gone mad? What about us then?"

Ali approached Mālik. He grabbed his shoulders tightly with both his hands. Mālik's eyes clearly betrayed his fear, and his shoulders were trembling. "I have every confidence that I can rely on you, but you can come with me, of course!"

He turned his head for a moment and looked at Sa'd and said, "You too, Sa'd; we can go together, the three of us."

"I will not go to a place where I know I will be defeated in battle. I do not have sufficient practice in dying. I have to rise higher than my brother."

Ali was surprised by Sa'd's words.

"Are you saying that the army of Ibn Ziād will be victorious?"

"That's right. There should be no doubt about it. My father says that if Husain ibn Ali does not surrender and does not pledge allegiance to Yazīd, Yazīd's army will be sent to Kūfa, and a hard battle will be fought!"

"Are you afraid of Yazīd's army?" asked Ali.

Sa'd's face turned dark. He always hated being called a coward. He couldn't help it. Ever since his older brother joined the Kūfa police and had reached the position of commander thanks to his record of good service, his father always criticized and belittled Sa'd. According to Sa'd's father, Sa'd was an incompetent and lazy child who could not even take care of his father's camels and caravans. For this reason, Sa'd trained hard to become a strong warrior so that he could take care of all his father's assets.

"How many fighters do you think there are in the Prophet's grandson's army? What's certain is that its number will not equal that of Yazīd's army." replied Sa'd.

Ali, who did not expect such a reaction from Sa'd was saddened by it. Mālik also turned silent, and in order to escape Ali's gaze, took what remained of his fish and gave it to Blacktail. Blacktail and his friend were frightened when they saw Mālik approaching and fled. Mālik threw what was left of his fish in their direction. Ali looked up at the sky. The sun was shining through some patches of white cloud. The waves of the Euphrates were rising higher than before. A strange and vague anxiety seemed to swell up in waves in the heart of the Euphrates. Ali looked at Saʻd and Mālik. Saʻd was taking off his long shirt.

"But I'm leaving. Nor should you talk to anyone about this." said Ali.

"I won't say anything." said Mālik.

"My mouth will remain closed, as always. And right now, I want to prove that I am not afraid of anything. We have to swim the race."

Ali looked at Saʻd in surprise. Saʻd took off his clothes and covered the lower half of his body with a piece of cloth. Ali looked at the waves and said, "I will accept losing the race. It is foolish to swim in these waves. I'd rather lose the race than drown."

Saʻd grinned and walked proudly towards the Euphrates with firm steps. When he reached the bank of the great river, the waves that were rising from the middle of the river swirled into each other and reached the shore. Saʻd felt the coolness of the water with his feet. The waves whipped at his legs one after another. They did not want him to enter the water.

"There is no one here to come to our aid if something should go wrong, and there will be nothing that Mālik and I will be able to do."

Sa'd gave Ali a mocking look and suddenly dived into the water. He laughed and plunged his head into the water and came back up and goaded Ali on. For a moment, Ali wanted to take off his clothes and join Sa'd in the water. Sa'd constantly boasted that he had become a warrior and could swim even in more violent waves. He wished that his father was there to see him so that he would praise him for his courage. His brother would surely be happy to hear about this news. Ali was debating with himself about what he should do. It did not matter to him anymore, of course. He might not see Sa'd anymore, and might only have to endure this victory of his a couple more times. It was at this point that Sa'd's boasting suddenly stopped. Ali looked worriedly at the water level to see Sa'd's head bob back up. Mālik was preoccupied with gathering his scattered herd again. Sa'd's head came up through the waves. He was struggling to stay afloat and was asking for help. The waves of the Euphrates had all conspired against him and were getting ready to devour him. They must have grown weary of the boasting of their uninvited guest. The sound of Sa'd's desperate cries for help had terrified the sheep. Blacktail was staring at the water with worry in his eyes, as was the white goat and the rest of the herd. Ali shouted loudly for Mālik to run to the village and get help. Mālik was in a state of panic. He had a look of desperation about him, until Ali shouted at him again and brought him to his senses. Mālik ran towards the village, and Sa'd's voice was getting muffled and drowned out. Ali was following Sa'd along the bank of the river as the current was taking him away and dived into the water after him. No matter how competitive they were, they never gave up on supporting each other. Until that moment, they had been angry with each other hundreds of times, but they thought of each other as brothers. And now Ali risked drowning so that he would remain loyal to his friends during their last days together.

A rider was riding at high speed on an agile black horse whose footsteps shook the ground violently. The village could be seen clearly from a distance. The horse raced so fast that it was as if its rider was bringing news of an impending attack.

Mālik was panting as he ran, and a large fat man in an expensive checkered suit who looked worried and stunned could be seen following behind him. Several men and women of the village could also be seen running after them, worried and upset. Perhaps the memory of several children drowning in the Euphrates earlier was on their minds. Was Sa'd also destined to become a part of the bitter memories of the Euphrates? His father ran with difficulty. He was distraught. His gaze was skyward as he continually asked God for help. How could any father reconcile himself with his son's death? He might have been strict, but that was only to make Sa'd grow up to be a good warrior. He knew very well that his eldest son would not be returning to the village, and that he was caught up with the longing for greater power. They eventually came upon the Euphrates and the herd of sheep next to it. Blacktail was standing and waiting for the people to arrive. He took to the riverbank and left as soon as he saw them, guiding the way for the others to follow him. The mute animal was taking them to two corpses. The half-naked bodies of Sa'd and Ali were lying on the muddy sands of the riverbank. Seeing that they were lifeless, Sa'd's father sat down on the ground right there and slapped the crown of his head hard with both hands. The Euphrates continued to roar and move forward. Its waves were still lashing at the bare feet of the children. Several men and women gathered around the father. He wailed and expressed his regret for being so strict with Sa'd. The rest of the villagers went towards the corpses.

That was when the sound of the two boys coughing up water was heard; they were alive! For the last time, Ali had managed to do a great service for his best friend and for the people of the village. He had dived into the heart of the waves and had managed to drag Sa'd back to the riverbank. They were shivering. The man on horseback who had rushed to the village and rousted the people, now joined the crowd. Everyone was happy. Sa'd and Ali's mothers hugged them both tightly. They smiled along with shedding tears that covered their cheeks and wiped their faces with the corners of their long shawls.

Sa'd's father, who was very relieved that the children were alive after all, suddenly came back to his usual self. Angry and upset, he got up and started reproaching Sa'd. Sa'd lowered his head when he heard his father's voice. The men of the village tried to calm his father down, but no one was a match for him. He shook the dust from his clothes and ran his hands over his face. He gave the children a reproachful look and headed towards the village, followed by the horseback rider. He was walking so fast that the rider could barely reach him. He pulled at the reins of his horse with one hand, and signaled Sa'd's father to stop with the other. Meanwhile, the rider's horse, who had barely caught its breath on the banks of the Euphrates, could not be coaxed to move. Eventually, Sa'd's father stopped.

"Are you the elder of this village and tribe?" asked the rider.

"Where are you from? What do you want with us?"

The rider, who was still trying to catch up with him with the same difficulty, said, "I have come from Kūfa. I have an important message from the palace of the governor."

Sa'd's father stopped moving. He paused for a moment, and then turned back to the rider anxiously.

The rider was happy to see Sa'd's father finally turn around. He could now catch his breath.

"What message did Ibn Ziād send to us?"

"It concerns Husain ibn Ali's caravan, which is headed for Kūfa."

Sa'd's father frowned.

He became worried and confused. What possible

request and message could Ibn Ziād have for him. He came closer to the rider, who had been followed by the villagers. Ali and Sa'd had been covered with robes. They could hardly walk; it was as if there was no life left in them. It was as if the Euphrates had suddenly swallowed them up and spat them out. "Join us. We will continue the conversation when we get home." said Sa'd's father. The rider followed them more easily. "I have visited several places since early this morning. I am very tired. I trust you will be a good host."

By the time they reached the village, the sun had risen to its zenith.

They had gathered in the large
courtyard of the house. Sa'd's father
had the rider enter first, and a slave
guided the horse with its reins to a stall
in the corner of the yard. The two
boys walked lifelessly, shivering to
their bones, even though they were
covered in felt robes. Their hair was still wet
and shone from the water of the Euphrates.
But as bad as the experience had been, it had ended
well; Sa'd's father understood this better than
everyone. He turned to the crowd and said,
"You are all guests in my house today.
I want to sacrifice a sheep in
gratitude for the boys' lives
having been spared."

The people looked at each other happily and a murmuring arose from their midst. The basis of their happiness had perhaps even more to do with the fact that now they could find out about the strange rider and his mission under the pretext of attending the party. They wanted to know who he was, where he came from, and more importantly, what his business was. Some of the elder menfolk made their way in, and the rest left, to return when the meal was to be served.

Umm Habīb was an old woman who stooped and walked with difficulty with the help of a wooden cane. She arrived at the house, concern showing on her face. Ali's mother and Mālik quickly made their way towards her. Umm Habīb's face was sunburned, and her white hair covered the wrinkles on her forehead. She had not taken off her black mourning attire since Mālik's father was martyred in Hujr ibn Udayy's uprising[1]. Her countenance was cold, and her large eyes and dark eyelids were lifeless.

The shadows of the leaves of the trees fell on the floor of the courtyard as if one was looking at a painting. Light made its way to the ground through the leaves. Several fat sheep that were constantly bleating had been

---

[1] Hujr Bin Udayy (Adī al-Kindī) was a companion of Imam Ali ﷺ who was killed by Mu'āwiya for refusing to curse Imam Ali ﷺ from the pulpit. Him and his associates were brutally massacred near Damascus.

tethered to the trees. There was a commotion in the yard. A big-boned slave was holding a large knife and was moving back and forth among the sheep.

Among all the slaves, there was one who commanded everyone's attention: the one who had prepared a large tray of food and drinks at the behest of Sa'd's father. The maids and slaves were whispering in his ear. It was clear what they were saying. They were asking him to listen carefully during the short period of time that he entered the room, to see what was being said, so that he could then come back and make his report and quench their curiosity. The slave in turn nodded his head up and down in response to their entreaties. He was finally released from the clutches of the other slaves' curiosity and left to himself.

Umm Habīb was busy pounding colorful medicinal herbs with a mortar and pestle on one of the large platforms in the courtyard. The strength of her hand was commendable given her slender body and old age. The mothers were sitting on the ground next to Umm Habīb. The mud and sand of the Euphrates still clung to their clothes and faces. Their eyes were red and even more lifeless than the two boys who had nearly drowned from all the crying and wailing they had done all the way from the village to the river. They looked at the two boys as if they had not seen them for a hundred years, or as if they had sent them off to war and they had now returned home safe and sound: or perhaps safe, but not so sound. Their bellies were still pounding, and they were still coughing, and their lungs were still in pain, but they did not utter a single word. They knew that once they opened their mouths, the reprimands would begin. But Mālik didn't care. Ali's sudden decision to go join Imam Husain ﷺ and Sa'd's foolish insistence on swimming in the dangerous waters of the Euphrates had weighed so heavily on his heart that he wanted to take his revenge on them. He constantly grumbled, "I *told* them! But no one listened to me. These two are crazy. Every day they get up to some dangerous act. They have to stay at home for a few days so that they learn to calm down."

Even Umm Habīb was surprised by the haughty words emanating from Mālik, which had made an impact on the way she was pounding the medicinal herbs with her pestle. The mothers shook their heads at the end of each groan and agreed to keep the boys at home for a few days.

Ali and Sa'd went to great lengths with the reproachful look they gave Mālik to finish his ranting, but Mālik refused to look their way and acted as if they didn't even exist.

The horse was the only one among them who was completely oblivious of everything; he had his head in the trough in a corner of his stable looking for some straw. He did not even raise his head to greet the other horses that were in the stable and were constantly neighing at him. It was clear from his eyes that he was tired. He must have wished that he was one of those horses. They did not leave the stables for weeks, but he had to travel for miles every day to carry a government official to report the news. And presently he found himself in the midst of these horses.

Now everyone knew that the strange rider was an official of the government in Kūfa. This was due to the spying efforts of that slave who was roaming the courtyard with a tray full of food. But no one knew on what business the man had come. The news from far and wide took its time to reach the villagers. News did not reach the village unless someone had returned from the Hajj pilgrimage, or unless one of Sa'd's father's caravans had returned from one of its trade runs, or if Sa'd's brother missed his hometown and returned to the village bringing the latest news with him. The last news that had reached the village was that Muslim ibn Aqīl, who had come on behalf of Husain ibn Ali ﷺ, had been arrested, and Ubaidullah had thrown him down from the roof of the governor of Kūfa's palace.

Umm Habīb finished her work and poured the powder of the mortar into two bowls and added a little water. The children were looking at her. Mālik took the two bowls at Umm Habīb's behest to give to the two boys.

Umm Habīb said in a muffled and tired voice, "Tell them to eat this; it is good for colic, stomach aches, and coughs."

Mālik glanced at the bowls. Their contents had a pungent, off-putting odor. He quickly took them to his two friends, who reluctantly took the bowls from him. Its appearance was unappetizing.

Everyone had their eyes peeled on the two boys and were waiting for them to eat up the medicine. It seemed there was no way to get out of it. Both of the boys' mothers, as well as Umm Ḥabīb, and worse than anyone else, Mālik, were all looking to make sure they took in the medicine. Ali and Saʿd raised their bowls at the same time. The mothers nodded in encouragement for the boys to quickly finish the medicine that was in the bowls. Saʿd finally took the medicine in, and Ali followed. Their faces fluttered from the bitterness and pungent smell of the medicine. Saʿd left the bowl half empty, but Ali ate it to the last drop. He was thinking that this incident of the water of the Euphrates making its way into his lungs might make him so ill and bedridden that he would no longer be able to follow his father and join Husain ibn Ali's ﷽ caravan, and that this regret would follow him for the rest of his life. He was so determined in his decision to join Husain ibn Ali's ﷽ caravan that he was willing to face even worse bitterness if he had to in order to achieve that aim.

Finally, after all that curiosity, Saʿd's father came out, followed by the rider. The rider had eaten so much that he could barely walk. His horse was not faring that much better either. Saʿd's father pointed to the stable hand and asked him to bring the rider's horse. The stable hand went to the stables immediately, took the horse by his reins, and brought him out.

Sa'd's father spoke jocularly with the rider and they both laughed as they approached the gate, Sa'd's father said, "I hope you were satisfied with the inadequate reception that we gave you at such short notice. We have a special devotion to the governor of Kūfa."

"Yes, your kindness exceeded my expectations."

A few slaves and handmaidens, and a few villagers who had remained behind under the pretext of seeing to the needs of the boys, and the boys themselves, looked with curiosity at Sa'd's father and at the rider. The sun was no longer at its peak. It was past noon. When they reached the door, Sa'd's father preceded him in honor of the envoy to Kūfa and opened the door himself instead of letting one of the slaves do so. When the door was opened completely, a tall, large man with a sunburned face stood in the doorway. The door was opened on him as he tried to knock on the door. He was out of breath and his face had turned red. He looked inside with concern. It was Habīb, Ali's father and Mālik's uncle. The one who wanted to leave at night with his friends and reach the caravan. When he heard that the children had fallen into the river, he had abandoned Sa'd's father's sheep in the desert and hurried to the village.

Sa'd's father broke out in a smile when he saw Habīb's face. For a moment, the rider and Ali's father looked at each other's faces. Sa'd's father extended his arms and went up to him, "Come, Habīb. You are welcome."

Habīb looked around anxiously and said in a muffled voice. "Wha… What about the boys?"

Sa'd's father hugged him tightly. This was the first time that Sa'd's father had hugged one of the villagers, and a shepherd of his flock at that.

"Do not worry about them. They are fine, praise God."

Habīb was not happy with Sa'd's father. Before Mālik's father was martyred in that uprising, Habīb was the general manager of Sa'd's father's caravans. He scouted the roads that his large caravans were to take and was responsible for the security of the caravans, which were always in danger. But as soon as he heard that Habīb's brother had been martyred in the Hujr ibn Udayy uprising, he dismissed Habīb for fear that his presence in his caravans might upset the government officials. In order not to upset Habīb, he had put him in charge of keeping his large flocks of sheep. He also always admitted that no one could match Habīb in the art of war and fighting off bandits. But conservatism was the primary principle he lived by.

Habīb stepped aside to let the rider pass. He had calmed down and knew that at least his son was alive. Ali's mother rushed toward him, but Habīb's eyes were also following the strange rider. He was a stranger, and everyone wondered who he was and where he had come from.

Sa'd's father returned after seeing the rider off and bidding him farewell. Ali's mother was whispering to his father. Habīb's countenance had become less concerned. Sa'd's father put his hand on Habīb's shoulder and said, "Your son did the greatest possible service for me today! If it were not for him, I would be mourning the death of my son."

Habīb's eyes sparkled with joy at hearing his son's courage being praised. He felt happy to the depth of his being. But the hearts of the boys became perturbed when they saw Habīb. They had forgotten all about swimming in the Euphrates and the story of their near drowning and the coming of the rider. They were all thinking about the words that had been exchanged between the three of them that morning before Sa'd dived into the water. Words that Habīb had set in motion. Sa'd and Mālik were staring at Ali's face, and Ali was looking back at them.

Habīb passed through the courtyard. He passed by the pots that were used in preparing the food for the banquet and came to a raised platform where the boys were seated. The boys stood up when they saw him. Habīb went up to Ali and pressed his hand firmly on his shoulder. He was excited. Habīb's hand was warm. Ali no longer felt the cold of the Euphrates that had previously pervading every inch of his body. Sa'd's father constantly praised Ali with loud words of praise and laughter, making his father very proud of his son. But a different passion stirred in Ali's heart. He was more confident now that he had grown up and could make big decisions.

During all this time, Sa'd had lowered his head. On one hand, Ali was his best friend and had saved his life from the danger of certain death, but on the other, this act of Ali's was tantamount to a lifelong stigma for his father, who could not even swim and whose son had to be saved by the son of their shepherd.

Although there were other elders in the village, because Sa'd's father was the richest man in the village and had many servants and trade caravans, he enjoyed the greatest status and respect. The rest of the population lived a mediocre life. Most of them were either Sa'd's father's shepherds or worked for him doing other things.

It was dusk. The sun was gradually giving way to the moon and stars. Slaves and handmaidens lit the oil lamps and distributed them between the menfolk and the womenfolk. They also lit the torches in the yard of every villager in turn. Children of all sizes were making a ruckus in the courtyard. The womenfolk were gathered on one side of the main building, and the menfolk had gathered in the main hall. All kinds of drinks and fruits were being served.

Children were sitting in a corner and talking where the menfolk had gathered in the main hall. Everyone was talking about the rider and the news he had brought with him. Sa'd's father kept repeating that he would give everyone the news from Kūfa after dinner had been served. But it is the mind's way to wander and to ask other questions. What was going on in Kūfa? What else happened after Muslim ibn Aqīl was put to death? Did Imam Husain's ﷺ caravan reached Kūfa, resulting in a battle breaking out? Is that why they had now sent an agent, to recruit soldiers? It was the same every time a war broke out: they came to the tribe and asked for soldiers due to the tribe's renowned for its warriors' fighting prowess. There was no end to the thoughts and imaginings that were expressed. But one thing was clear. Sa'd's father would stare into space and go deep into thought every time Kūfa was mentioned.

The situation was completely different in the women's gathering. Sa'd's and Ali's mothers told the story of the morning and the near drowning of their boys. Each time they repeated the story, they added more details and stated the facts with greater exaggeration. The women were paying rapt attention to what they were saying. They said that God had shown great mercy in giving their sons back to them again. Then, a mother whose son had drowned in the Euphrates the previous year, began to wail. It took a lot of hard work and time for them to be able to comfort her and calm her down. When you have a combination of a river that is so large and briming with waves of water, and when there are children who love to swim and sometimes compete, then there will be times when such accidents will happen. It is the Euphrates, after all. Its presence necessarily brings with it the risk of people drowning, and its absence equates to the absence of life.

The tablecloths were spread and filled with plates full of meat and rice and stews. The spread was so colorful that even the moon was impressed, to the point that she shone like the light of a thousand oil lamps.

Sa'd was looking to get Ali alone. Mālik had been clinging on to them since the morning. Sa'd did not want Mālik to hear him thanking Ali. When all was said and done, he was Sa'd, with all of the pride which that entailed. Ali got up from the table spread and went out, and Mālik was so busy eating that he did not notice.

Ali was standing by a tree under the moonlight and a canopy of stars. Ali was lost in his thoughts again. He was lost in thoughts of leaving and following his father and his father's friends when Sa'd's voice brought him back down to earth. He had come to thank Ali. His eyes were downcast, as he was ashamed. Perhaps he had never had to thank anyone before or had not done so because of his personality; but this time it was different. Ali had pulled him back from certain death. If the Euphrates swallowed him up, there would have been nothing he could have done. So, he needed to thank Ali, even if it was just a cursory "thank you" and nothing else.

Ali came forward and stood next to him. He stared into Sa'd's eyes and smiled, "You are my best friend, Sa'd! There's no need to thank me; we are brothers. Can there be anything higher than this?!"

Tears came to Sa'd's eyes. Ali gave him a big hug, at which point Mālik joined them, "What are you up to? Are you planning on doing something else to make us miserable?"

Both chimed, "No."

Then Ali and Sa'd looked at each other and smiled mischievously.

"Come back inside. Sa'd's father is about to let everyone know why the rider from Kūfa came here." Mālik then gave them a smile and went inside. That was how Mālik was; his heart was as big as the sea itself. But he was easily upset too.

By now everyone had eaten their food and the tables had been cleared. Everyone was so full they could barely talk. Most of them were shepherds who usually slept early and were not used to staying up late. These kinds of nights occurred maybe once or twice a year.

Sa'd's father slowly began to speak. Everyone was listening with rapt attention. Habīb was sitting beside him. Everyone was silent, from the elders of the village to the little boys.

"Today we had a guest from the Government in Kūfa.[2] He brought us a message from Ubaidullah."

---

[2] In those days, Kufa was a garrison town and the provincial capital of a vast region that covered most of the former Persian empire – translator.

People started whispering to each other. Everyone knew this and was silent again once Sa'd's father motioned them to be quiet.

"Husain ibn Ali has refused to pledged allegiance to the Commander of the Faithful Yazīd and is moving towards Kūfa."

Everyone's ears perked up, especially Habīb's and Ali's.

"Ubaidullah killed his envoy Muslim ibn Aqīl and executed Hāni ibn Urwa on the charge that he gave Muslim refuge, even though Hāni was the chief of the Madhhaj tribe. And presently, anyone who is seen providing the slightest bit of assistance to Husain ibn Ali is arrested. All of you should know that soldiers have been positioned on all the roads coming in and out of Kūfa. Ubaidullah has sent couriers to all the tribes and villages and towns in the vicinity warning them that anyone thinking of helping Husain ibn Ali will be severely punish, along with his tribe."

Many of the people present had been frightened by this kind of talk. Some were talking with each other, and Habīb was deep in thought, and Ali was looking at his father furtively.

Sa'd's father continued, "I know that the preservation of the village and tribe's security is each and every one of our priorities. We have established this life of ours here with the blood of our hearts and with much work and effort. So, each of you should take full responsibility for your own behavior as well as that of the people around you. I do not want anyone from our village to even think of joining our Prophet's grandson's caravan. Doing so would make our whole village an enemy in the eyes of the Umayyads and the Commander of the Faithful Yazīd!"

A buzz arose from the gathered crowd. Everyone was saying something. Some agreed and some disagreed. The ruckus was so great that one could not discern what the individual voices were saying. Sa'd's father clapped his hand several times, after which the noise subsided.

Sa'd's father continued, "This was the message delivered today by Ubaidullah's courier. Everyone should know that I will arrest and imprison anyone who is entertaining thoughts of joining up with Husain ibn Ali's forces, in order to protect our village and our people. I will then hand over the prisoners to the forces of the government in Kūfa."

The faces of Habīb and his friends became pale. And the boys exchanged anxious glances with each other. Thoughts were coming to each of their minds in waves. But no one was as worried as Mālik and Sa'd. They were very concerned about Ali, about whose plans no one, not even his father, knew anything about; it was unclear how he could follow his father in order to join Husain ibn Ali's ﷺ caravan with all of the precautions that were now in place. The task had become many times more difficult for his father and his father's friends, let alone for someone who intended to secretly follow them.

3

Night had fallen, and the sound of crickets filled the courtyard. The stars were sparkling brilliantly in the dense canopy they formed over the village. Everywhere was lit up by moonlight. Light shone through the all-wooden window frames of the main room. Male slaves and handmaidens were moving back and forth, collecting all the dishes and crockery that had been used at the party. Sa'd was sitting in a corner, thinking. All the guests were gone. A voice in Sa'd's mind constantly beckoned him. Because of what Sa'd's father had said, he was now thought of by the boys as being a coward who was willing to give up members of his own tribe to face the possibility of being put to death, for fear of what the government might do to him. These were the kinds of thoughts that some of the men of the tribe had given expression to in their whisperings, and which Ali had expressed personally to Sa'd. And he was right: fear had taken over Sa'd's father's entire being. He never did anything to jeopardize his position. He always triangulated, as if with a pair of calipers, which army would be victorious, and threw his support to that side. And he already knew what fate awaited Husain ibn Ali ☽ and his caravan, now that the people of Kūfa had abandoned him and deprived him of their support.

But these words were not acceptable to Sa'd's mind. He was a proud boy whose pride had been completely shattered twice since yesterday morning. And on both occasions, this occurred in front of someone who had been defeated on numerous occasions. Ali's image did not leave his eyes even for a single moment. He walked slowly and with deliberation, like a champion who has been deprived of all his medals at once in a single day. When he reached the foot of the wooden-framed window, he could clearly hear his father's voice. He was angry.

"Do you think that you will listen to what I have just said merely because of my just having said it? But I know the mentality of you people!"

Sa'd then heard the voices of the elders and those among the people who had not yet left the gathering, "When Ibn Ziād says that he will punish us, what he is really saying is that he will destroy us. You have not forgotten what his father did to the poor people of Basra, have you?"

Sa'd's father could be heard, "We have to make sure that no one can leave the village; that the thought of such a thing does not even occur to anyone."

Another elder asked, "How can such a thing be done? Are you going to put everyone's legs in leg irons?? Why does Ubaidullah not send his own forces to ensure the compliance of the villages and tribes?"

"That's right. As soon as the name of our prophet's grandson is mentioned, they draw their swords out!", said another.

"We should not allow this. We must be very careful. You understand what I am talking about...", said S'ad's father.

An elder suggested, "I for one say that you should imprison everyone you suspect. Ubaidullah is indeed to be feared! Do you remember what his father did to those who were sympathetic to Ali ibn Abī Tālib? This is the son of that same father!"

Presently a familiar voice responded to everyone's comments. His voice sounded familiar to Sa'd. It was the voice of the person who was in charge of all of his father's caravans; it was the voice of the person who had replaced Habīb. He was brawny, and although he looked kind, he had a heart of stone. Nor did he fool around. In fact, he had grabbed Sa'd's ear and twisted it on more than one occasion. His name was Amr, and he had lost his father in the war that was waged against the Iranians.

"Leave it to me. I will make sure that no one who can make a move in this village makes a move without my being informed about it."

A shiver ran through Sa'd's whole body for a brief moment. When Amr spoke, he meant what he said, and his words would be borne out by reality. He had informants throughout the village among the shepherds, and even, some believed, among the dogs! On several occasions when Sa'd's father's camels had disappeared, he himself had delved into the matter and taught the shepherds who had stolen the camels a good lesson. Now Habīb and his friends could not make a move without Amr knowing about it. The thought of the men who wanted to slip away from the village falling into Amr's hands occupied the entirety of Sa'd's mind.

His mind was so preoccupied that he did not realize when his father's secret meeting was over and that the guests had come out. These consisted of some elders who were walking with canes, and Amr, who put a hand on Sa'd's shoulder and gave him a smile as he said goodbye. Amr had talked to Sa'd on many occasions, especially after he put an idea into Sa'd's father's mind and used his older brother against him. He would say that Sa'd should do things to make himself more popular than his brother in his father's eyes. But this was impossible; for how could be compete with his brother?! His brother was the head of the Kūfa police and enjoyed the favors of the governor of Kūfa! But Sa'd was just a boy whose skills could be summed up in his ability to wrestle, ride on horseback, and swim. And now, with that swimming disaster that had befallen him, he could no longer count swimming as part of his skill set.

When the guests left, his father returned. His father's eyes fell on Sa'd, who was still standing under the wooden window-frame, wincing. His father emptied all of his frustrations of the day wholesale onto Sa'd: from the near-drowning misadventure of the morning and the courage displayed by Habīb's son, to the arrival of the rider from the Kūfa governorate. But Sa'd was only there in body and not in spirit. He did not hear anything. He was looking for a way to put an end to all this. His father did his usual grumbling, but when he saw that Sa'd did not respond, and just stood there like a mute boy, he shook his head as if he felt sorry for him and went inside. But Sa'd stayed where he was.

Just like the night before, Ali could not sleep, and his sleeplessness had made him restless. Everyone was asleep, but Ali occupied himself with petting the white goat in a corner of the courtyard, petting him so much that the goat ended up sleeping peacefully in his arms. The hesitation and ambivalence he felt last night was gone. What he was worried about was that his father and his friends might change their minds because of what Sa'd's father had said. Habīb refrained from involving himself in such issues since his uncle had been martyred because of his consideration of how Umm Habīb was feeling. All of the people who worked in Sa'd's father's caravan wanted Habīb to be reappointed as their manager. Sometimes they would come to Sa'd's father and beseech him to save them from Amr's menace. Many of the caravan sentinels had quit their jobs forever because they did not get paid enough money to put up with Amr. But life had its expenses, which they strove to provide for by shepherding, swordsmanship, snooping, or trade.

All these thoughts swirled around Ali's mind and slowly enabled his eyelids to close, and let sleep overtake him as he was sitting in the corner of the courtyard hugging the white goat who was also asleep.

Sa'd paced the courtyard all night. His mother had come to the door to the courtyard several times to look in on him. She thought that he was unable to sleep due to his father's reprimands, but the truth was something else. A thought had occurred to him, and he was not able to distinguish between whether it was a good or a bad thing. He kept pacing the yard and telling himself, "I will save them, and by doing so, I will save myself." He kept repeating this as he continued to pace the yard. The sound of stray dogs could be heard, but even their barking and howling didn't have any effect on Sa'd.

Gradually the stars in the sky lost their luster and faded away. Traces of the sun's golden rays gradually appeared in the sky. Sa'd was standing by the door, waiting for his family to wake up for the morning prayer. His father was usually the first to get up. He opened the door and came into the courtyard. When he saw Sa'd, he shook his head again in pity. Sa'd didn't say anything; all he did was to look to his father to see what he did. Sa'd's father offered his ritual devotions, and he went to lay back down and sleep, but Sa'd called him before he did so. At first, he wanted to ignore him, but Sa'd called him again. He then looked at Sa'd reproachingly. But Sa'd spoke up before his father could start on his usual tirade of reproaches.

"I know of something that you are unaware of."

He had not paced the courtyard all night in vain, and what he was saying was not delusional. The thoughts that had occurred to him at night would not leave him alone.

"Why has your tongue stopped?

What is it that you know about that I am not aware of??" snapped his father.

Sa'd was ambivalent and was stuck as to whether or not to say what he had started to say. He stuttered a little, and then decided to come out with it. He said, "Ali's father and his friends want to go."

His father suddenly got up and said, "Go where??"

Now his father was standing right in front of Sa'd. Sa'd was holding his breath, which felt trapped in his chest.

"They want to join forces with Husain ibn Ali!"

His father laughed out loud, making light of this news, but he was worried, and his hands were shaking.

"How do you know this?! Do you think that you can make up for yesterday's disaster by making up these kinds of things? You're just saying this so to make Habīb look bad in my eyes!"

"No, by God, I - I'm telling the truth! I heard it from Ali myself. He wants to follow his father too!"

This gave his father pause.

If anyone from their tribe went to join

forces with the caravan of the Prophet's grandson, everything he had would be endangered. Sa'd was waiting. It was as if someone was telling him in his heart that what he had done was not a good thing. This feeling multiplied when his father asked him to do something that was the worst possible thing in the world that he could have asked him to do.

He wanted him to hurry to Habīb's house and to tell him to come to see his father before he left his house for the desert. Sa'd wanted to say something and make his father send someone else to do what he had been asked to do. But his father's demand was so firm that it sent a wave of fear through Sa'd, who knew that he had no choice but to accept it and carry it out.

The sheep came out of the stable one at a time. The sheep dog was barking. Mother and Umm Habīb had a pail in which they milked the sheep that were brought out by Mālik and Ali. The sound of the bleating of the sheep pervaded the whole village. Sa'd's father's herd was so large that it stayed in a special camp in the desert. Ali's father was getting ready to head out to the desert. The white goat was playing with Ali's little sister Samā. The pails were gradually filled with milk and then emptied into a larger container. Ali's body ached all over. He constantly rubbed his neck with his hands.

Sa'd was on his way. An inner voice constantly reproached him. He had revealed the secret of his best friend. If his friends saw him, they would know that he had informed on Ali to his father. He talked to himself, trying to justify what he had done. Ali was his best friend. He could not let Ali follow his father so that Ubaidullah's soldiers would arrest him and imprison and torture him… Certainly, in that event, Ali, like his father and his father's friends, would not come out of this alive. It was true that by giving this news to his father he had increased his favor in his father's eyes; and true, it was possible that his father would forget yesterday's disaster altogether, but his intention was not only to benefit himself. He stated these words and passed by the mud and straw outer walls of the village, on the other side of which were houses that were not very large. When he neared Ali's house, he saw his friends milking the sheep. They would not leave until the task of milking had been completed. He stood in a corner waiting for them to leave. He was afraid to go forward. But he saw that Habīb was getting ready to leave. If Habīb left, he would have to return empty-handed to his father, and would hear his father rebuke him again. So he had to finish what he had started. He gathered all his courage and set off.

The sheep who had already been milked were waiting outside the doorway in their own orderly manner. None of them was as preoccupied with his own whims as the white goat. He passed between them and reached the door, which was set in a large wooden frame. Mālik was preoccupied with one of the goats, holding him by its horns and pulling him along. Ali had taken hold of a goat and was holding it for his mother, who was milking it. His father was tying the laces of his boots, which were like those worn by soldiers before battle. Everyone was taken aback for a moment to see Sa'd greet him. Mālik let go of the horns of the unfortunate goat and stared at Sa'd. Ali just stared at him, dumbfounded. What was Sa'd doing there so early in the morning? Habīb tightened the laces of his boots and stood in front of Sa'd.

Habīb asked, "Salaam alaykum. What brings you here this early in the morning? Has something happened?"

Sa'd's hands and heart were trembling, and his voice was even worse.

"No... my father wanted to see you."

Suddenly, Ali's face turned pale. Mālik looked over at Ali.

"Do you not know what business he has with me?"

Now Sa'd increased Ali and Mālik's suspicion. They became more concerned, and Sa'd's voice trembled even more.

"I don't know. He just said he needed to talk to you about something."

Habīb, who was unaware of what was going on, thought it had something to do with the shepherding of the herd again. Habīb said goodbye to everyone and told Ali and Mālik to tend to the sheep. The boys just nodded their heads without being able to say anything. Habīb set off, and Sa'd did not want to face his friends at that moment, preferring to have to explain to them what had happened at a more appropriate time. Of course, the anxiety that showed in his eyes and the worry that was all around him had revealed everything. Sa'd said goodbye with a wave of his hand and followed Habīb. Ali and Mālik abandoned the sheep and followed after Sa'd as quickly as the wind. Ali's mother and Umm Habīb exchanged glances. They were worried about Ali and Mālik's behavior. Samā hugged the white goat to her chest and followed them.

Habīb was walking ahead, taking long strides, and Sa'd was following a few steps behind him. Ali snuck up and grabbed Sa'd, putting his hand over his mouth from behind, and pulled him aside, taking him by surprise. There was fear and apprehension in Ali's trembling face and voice!

"What business does your father have with my father? Why has he sent you for him??"

Sa'd took a deep breath, and looked at Ali and Mālik, then said, "I don't know anything other than the fact that my father wanted me to come after him!"

Mālik gave a grimace and said, "You think we are idiots?! Your father, with all his slaves, should send *you* after my uncle??"

Suddenly, Mālik angrily grabbed Sa'd by his collar. It was as if he wanted to crush all of his bones into dust. Habīb was the only refuge Sa'd had left. When his father was martyred, their house had been set on fire. If his uncle had not brought him back with him, he would undoubtedly be begging in the streets of Kūfa and sleeping on the street at night.

Mālik growled, "tell the truth! Why have you turned so pale?"

Ali removed Mālik's hands from Sa'd's collar with great difficulty.

"Sa'd, tell me the truth, what happened? What possible business could your father have with my father after everything he said last night?"

Sa'd straightened his collar with his hands. It was all over. He had to tell the truth. After all, he mostly did it to save Ali. So, what was there for him to be afraid of?

"I did this to save you!"

Ali and Mālik's eyes widened in surprise.

"Did what??"

Now Ali and Mālik were convinced they knew what Sa'd had done. But they did not want to believe it.

Now, if Sa'd's father said something, Habīb would surely understand what Ali had in mind, and would not allow him to go with him if only for the sake of his family. Apart from his own large family and Umm Habīb, Habīb also supported Mālik and his sisters. Someone had to stay behind to help support the family. Now Ali was hot under the collar. Beads of sweat ran down his face. This time it was he who grabbed Sa'd's collar and hit him on the face so hard that it made Sa'd to cry out in pain.

"You revealed my plan!"

He beat Sa'd unrelentingly. Sa'd did not want to hit him back. Finally, in the depths of his conscience, he admitted that he had wronged Ali, although his intentions had been good.

"Tell me now, what exactly is it that you said? Speak up!!"

Ali had never before been so angry. Mālik had become afraid of his earnestness and his anger. He was truly crushing Sa'd with everything he had. When Mālik saw that Ali could not control his anger, he took hold of him and pulled him off Sa'd, who pulled himself together and got up with some difficulty. Ali's eyes were red with rage, and his body burned like a raging furnace. His having put his trust in Sa'd in telling him of his father's plan was the worst mistake he had ever made in his life.

"Let him be let's go see what's going on."

Sa'd cursed everyone inside. He wiped the blood from his nose with a corner of his sleeve and patted the dirt off his clothes. He followed behind Ali and Mālik, talking to them all the time. But Mālik would not let Ali turn back. One of the things he said was that he did this because Amr had become responsible for spying on everyone, and that he was to arrest anyone who displayed any kind of suspicious activity, and he undoubtedly had become aware of Ali's father's plans. He said that he told his father about the plan in order to curtail the matter and prevent things from getting worse. The boys eventually arrived at Sa'd's home. Ali turned and looked at Sa'd. What he was saying with his looks was that Sa'd should invite them into his home. Sa'd went ahead and opened the door. All three stood behind a wooden-framed window and listened.

A slight sound could be heard. It was as if two people were quietly whispering something. Ali asked Mālik to weave his fingers together so that his hands would act as a step so Ali could step up and listen at the window. But Sa'd intervened and asked them to follow him.

They climbed a wooden ladder that was in a corner of the courtyard up to the roof. The roof was full of mats that were spread out in the yard for people to sit on. A few camel and horse saddles were also lying in a corner. Sa'd led his friends up to a wooden portico which was in the corner of the large room and had been covered with palm fronds. Sa'd pushed the palm fronds aside quickly and opened the window that opened to the outside. Now the sound could be heard clearly.

"Habīb, you are a good man. I have not yet forgotten the fate that befell your brother. I do not want the same fate to befall you!"

"What are you talking about? Has something happened?"

Mālik's eyes filled with tears when he heard this.

Sa'd used this feeling to say, "There, Mālik! That's the fate I did not want Ali to be caught up in too. So, was I wrong to try to prevent it??"

Ali became more upset and frowned.

Sa'd's father said, "No. It's just that I thought that you might think of doing something you might regret because of your love for the Family of the Prophet."

Ali calmed down a little when he heard Sa'd's father's words, which had not revealed what had given rise to the incident. He went to the edge of the roof and did not wait for his father to leave the room. Sa'd was concerned that Ali might do something. But instead, all Ali did was take Mālik by the hand and quickly leave the yard. Sa'd followed them. He called out to them two or three times, but they did not pay any attention to him. When they entered the alley, Sa'd ran and caught up with them and stood in front of them.

"Wait, I need to talk to you."

Ali pushed him aside with his hand and passed him by.

"I will have nothing to do with cowards. You are a coward, just like your father! You think I don't know how much this snitching of yours has endeared you to your father?"

"You're mistaken!"

Ali's emotions weighed heavily on him, and he talked constantly. Mālik was in a different mood. He was again remembering the words they had spoken about his father.

"As of today, we are no longer friends. You broke our pact of friendship! If your father were to reveal my plans, I would do something to you so that you would no longer be able to speak another word, let alone inform on people!"

Sa'd was stunned by Ali's words, and he just stood there and looked at him, and all he could do is bite his lip in anger.

Now Ali and Mālik moved away from him with long strides, and before long Sa'd voice no longer reached them. Ali's father came out of the door at the same time Ali arrived. His face was a little worried, but he was so firm and in control that he behaved very normally. Only Sa'd, who knew what plans he had in mind, could feel a hint of his concern.

When Sa'd entered the house, his father was standing in the courtyard. He was happy. It was the first time that Sa'd's father had a smile on his face when he looked at him, instead of a reproachful frown. Suddenly his father started to clap his large, powerful hands, and his voice echoed in the courtyard and in Sa'd's ears. This was an act of encouragement and approval of his father's for which he had given up something precious.

"I knew that one day my own blood would show up in my son's veins. You did a great thing today."

Sa'd was overwrought by feelings of guilt and remorse, and all he could manage was a faint artificial smile. His father praised him even more than he was used to praising his older brother. There was no end to the praise that he lavished on him. His praises were like the golden rays of the sun, which got brighter and brighter at every passing moment.

Ali and Mālik were occupied with each other for the rest of the day. Ali grumbled, and Mālik tried to calm him down, after which Mālik would complain, and this time Ali was the one who tried to assuage him. Neither of them wanted to believe that Sa'd had snitched on them and that a big argument had taken place between them. It seemed that even the white goat did not have the motivation to run away; he was sitting quietly by a tree. It was as if all of Ali's anxieties and concerns had spread to the goat on the night he had slept in Ali's arms. Even the fish of the Euphrates River, which were reprieved by Mālik the previous day, were restless and kept jumping in and out of the water. Maybe they missed Mālik and were challenging him to a good struggle between them.

As for Sa'd, he just walked around the house like a chicken with his head cut off. He had nothing in particular that he had to do. Sometimes he went horseback riding. But riding without having any friend and competitor was not satisfying. He felt lonely. He wanted to go to his friends on several occasions, but each time he remembered Ali's blows, his calling him and his father cowards, and worst of all, calling him a snitch. When he remembered these things, resentment and hatred pervaded his whole being. But what was to become of all this ultimately? They couldn't remain angry at each other forever.

4

One day had passed since Sa'd had informed on his friends to his father. Mālik, as always, was lying on the bank of the Euphrates, trying his luck at fishing. The fish were used to it too. Every time they heard his voice, they would recognize it and dive deeper into the water. But every once in a while, one of them who didn't know the little fisherman of the Euphrates would swim up and get caught in his hook.

The sheep dog was up to his usual mischief again with his friend. It was a good way for passing the time; it got him out of his loneliness, and most importantly, if a wolf ever came close to the sheep, the two of them could confront him together. How often he had wished for his friend to become a sheep dog too so that his friend could work with him and under his supervision. The white goat jumped up and down, playing with one of the lambs, jumping over the sheep that were lying down and basking in the sun, making them grumble for not being left in peace. There was just one thing that was unusual in all this. Ali was sitting under a tree, having turned his back on the herd. He was honing down a piece of wood that he held in his hand and was shaping it into a saber with a knife he held in his hand. He was so strong that the piece of wood had started to complain too, and constantly slipped out of his hands and fell to the ground. His mind was not on what he was doing, nor was he thinking about roasting Mālik's fish. It was as if he was expecting something. He missed Sa'd, despite the brawl that he had started between them. He turned his head and looked at every sound that he heard. His mind was so preoccupied that he had forgotten to bring their bundle of bread this morning.

Samā was holding the bundle under one of her arms and holding one hand over her eyes to shield them from the light of the sun. She had large eyes with long eyelashes that betrayed her mischievous nature. She was thinking of a way to make an excuse to stay with her brother. Maybe she could have some fun all day with the white goat along the shore of the Euphrates instead of working at home. Whenever she got tired of staying at home, she would sneak out to find Ali, and Ali didn't have the heart to tell her to go back and would let her play with the white goat and the other lambs until it was time to head back home. She had climbed up some of the palm trees on several occasions too. The first time she did this, Ali encouraged her, but Mālik had frightened her so much that she became frozen where she stood, and Ali had had to go up to her and grab her and make their way down together. But now she had become a master at climbing. Ali got up suddenly as soon as he saw someone approaching. It was not clear who it was. He thought it was Sa'd, who had come to apologize. But when he saw it was Samā when she came closer, he was disappointed and sat back down.

Ali had gotten bored. The sun was now right in the middle of the sky, and their wooden swords were lying on the ground on the side of the mound where they played, which was now vacant. For Ali, no one could take Sa'd's place. He suddenly vented all of his frustrations by yelling at his sister.

The little girl just stood there, mute; too shocked to say anything. Even Mālik, who did not like girls being around them very much, let a fish that was on his hook back in the water upon hearing Ali's loud yelling. The white goat came up to Samā. The dogs were taken aback; it was as if they were pinned to the ground like statues. Samā began to cry. She hadn't done anything, she thought; all she wanted to do is play. Ali put his hands on his head and sat on the ground next to the tree. Samā hugged the white goat and ran away. As she was leaving, she said, "The fool has had an argument with Sa'd and is taking it out on me. You deserve to have Sa'd make you miserable!"

Upon hearing these words, Ali involuntary lowered his hands from his head momentarily. Mālik, who had come to mediate, was shocked by the words of the mischievous little girl!

"What did she say??"

Ali understood what had happened. Samā had followed them that day and seen them fighting. Now he had to worry about this new development too. If Samā felt like going with Ali, there was nothing he could do about it. Mālik struck him lightly on his head with both hands and said, "As if Sa'd wasn't enough to worry about! Now what are you doing to do about this little tyke?"

Ali gathered his thought, and said, "Samā is an intelligent girl."

Mālik grinned and said, "This is what comes of a girl who climbs trees! Where did she take the goat?!"

Ali ignored Mālik's words and took up the wooden sword and started to whittle away at it again.

When Mālik saw that Ali was not paying any attention to him, he went to the little bundle that Samā had thrown on the ground. It was full of fresh hot bread. He looked at the loaves of bread and raised his head up for a moment. It was lunch time.

"Even the bread has arrived, but I still haven't caught a single fish."

There was a commotion in the courtyard of Sa'd's house. A caravan of camels was lined up and the slaves were lowering their packs to the ground. One by one, chests and carpets and high-quality fabrics were placed on the platform. Sa'd's father viewed the goods with a smile on his face. Amr walked between the camels and inventoried their loads. This was one of Sa'd's father's smallest caravans. Although Sa'd's father could build a large and magnificent palace in Kūfa or even in the Levant with the wealth that he had, he did not want to leave the village. He had repeatedly asked Amr to tell him about the Umayyad Mosque and palace and had decided to build a mosque and a palace like theirs in the village. His eldest son was opposed to this and wanted him to do this in Kūfa so that his status would be raised and so that they would be relieved of the hardships of life in the village.

As usual, Sa'd was hanging around in the midst of the caravan. He could never be trusted with the responsibility of any important task. He had often dreamed of being able to work like a trader who was trusted by his father, and to make a living for himself in that way. Only Mālik and Ali knew why he learned riding and swordsmanship and why he practiced so hard at them. In fact, there was no real competition between the two brothers, because his older brother had a position in the government and Sa'd wanted to become a rich and powerful trader. And the grooms of the family each held a position in the business operations of this rich villager. But having been compared too much with his older brother made Sa'd aspire to reach a point higher than his brother and to sit on a throne on the peak of the wealth of his father.

Sa'd's father looked around and saw that Sa'd was delighted to see a high-quality sword among the goods that had arrived with the caravan, and that he was trying it out by turning the sword in his hand. He called out to Sa'd, who became concerned as to why he was being summoned by his father. But this time it was different. He could not believe that this time, his father asked him to take charge of storing the caravan's goods. Sa'd became excited and quickly went to work at his assigned task. His father was watching him; and for his part, Sa'd kept giving orders, like a warlord. He did not let the work stop, even for a moment. In the meantime, Amr came and stood behind Sa'd's father. He looked at Sa'd and smiled.

"This son of yours takes after you. You might be able to count on him for even bigger tasks."

Sa'd's father nodded his head and said, "If he listens to what I say, why not! He is just like me."

Ali was sent to fetch Salman, a middle-aged man who had previously worked in the caravans. Many caravans hired him because of his knowledge of medicine, but he had lost his motivation to work since he lost his wife to an illness on his way back from the Hajj pilgrimage. He had a small house in the village where he worked. Ali knocked on the door. The smell of wild mountain medicinal herbs and of the herbal remedies he kept wafted around the house. It was night and everywhere was dark. There was no moon in the night sky. It was only the light of the stars that reached the earth and lit the way for Ali, who was holding Salman's belongings in his hands and taking long strides.

"Where did this occur?!"

"In the desert... he has been moaning since he came back." said Ali.

"Did he send you after me himself?"

"It was mostly on Umm Habīb's insistence. She said she didn't understand what the problem was and that it would be better to fetch you."

Salman thought for a moment and looked around. In the sheer darkness of the village alleys, someone was following them every step of the way, but stopped doing so after they had reached a certain point.

Several people were talking in the courtyard of Amr's house at night. Amr was standing among them. They had lit a fire. One of them stirred the coals with a long, thin stick.

One of the men said, "He was moaning when he came. His hand was on his stomach."

"Did you hear what was wrong with him?", asked Amr.

"No. The shepherds said that he could no longer remain in the desert after he ate some food. So, his son went to fetch Salman."

"Wasn't Umm Habīb around?"

"His son told Salman she said she could not cure him."

Amr started at the fire for a moment.

"Do not leave Habīb but be on your guard for the others."

Habīb was in pain. He was moaning. Umm Habīb was sitting next to his head. The whole family was gathered around him. When Salman and Ali arrived, Habīb asked everyone to leave. Even Umm Habīb left the room. Ali and Mālik were standing outside the door. Umm Habīb wanted them to pay close attention so that if Salman wanted something, they could get it. But Ali and Mālik heard some strange things being said.

Habīb, in a hushed voice said, "The caravan was not allowed to enter Kūfa; they have decamped not far from here. Can you believe it?"

"In that case, there is no longer a problem for our departure. We'll be able to leave at night; no one will see us leave in the dark."

As he was saying these words, Habīb looked around the room and let out some moans. He was worried that if Umm Habīb found out, she would prevent him from leaving.

"It is not that simple. All the roads have been closed, and they arrest everyone they see. One of the members of the caravan was saying that they wanted to force the grandson of the Prophet to pledge his allegiance."

"That is not possible. If he was not averse to pledging his allegiance, he would have stayed in Medina." said Salman.

Ḥabīb shook his head in disapproval of the whole situation.

But he had unknowingly gladdened Ali's heart. He was relieved that the plan of his father and his father's friends was still intact. What was more, his father's ingenuity in the way he brought this secret meeting about with Salman, who had easier access to everyone due to the nature of his work, made him feel good too. But Mālik was worried. There was fear and apprehension in his eyes. When their ears were focused on hearing the words that were being spoken, Ali's eyes fell on Samā. She was just standing there with here diminutive stature and looking at them as would a creditor. Mālik, who saw her, said, "This half-pint knows more about what's going on than me!"

Suddenly he frowned to scare her off, and said, "What are you doing here, little girl? Are you looking to get a spanking?"

Samā made herself look all innocent and shook her head no. Ali realized that if they got on Samā's wrong side, she might say something to her father or to Umm Ḥabīb. So, he gave her a smile and slowly went and sat down next to her. Now he was only a few inches taller than her. He placed a hand on Samā's shoulder and stroked her long black wavy hair.

"Are you my sister or Sa'd's?!"

Samā was a little taken aback. She looked at Mālik, who had his ear to the door and was listening in.

"I'm your sister... Sa'd and Mālik are little devils!"

Ali laughed at Samā's words. Although Mālik's attention was on what he was hearing from the room, he heard what Samā said and frowned at her.

Ali took Samā's hands and said, "If you can be a good girl and not tell anyone that Sa'd and I had a fight, I'll give you something nice."

Samā's eyes sparkled with excitement. She threw herself in Ali's arms. Ali was taken by surprise momentarily. He thought about how much Samā loved him, and how his absence would surely bring tears to the eyes of the little girl who was embracing him at this moment because of her passion and love for him.

The party was ready to leave. Everything was done in secret and without any overt communication with each other due to their fear of what Sa'd's father would do. Salman carried out much of the communication and necessary planning as he was less likely to be suspected.

Mālik and Ali talked under the light of the stars after Salman left. Habīb's plans were something new to them. Mālik was heartbroken. He said that after Ali and his uncle left, he would no longer have the heart and mind to continue living, and that he would no longer know how to carry on living. He talked a little about Umm Habīb and Ali's mother, and what they would do when they found out that Ali had left with his father. But unlike Mālik, Ali was merely thinking what he was going to take with himself when he left. They would be on the move for two more nights. Sometimes the thought occurred to Ali to somehow get hold of a horse and make his way over to Kūfa on his own. But then he changed his mind and thought that he would be risking ruining his father's plan if he did so.

Ali fell asleep before Mālik did. Mālik's mind was walking among the stars. He thought to himself that his father was like a star in the heavens. Umm Habīb always said that his father had risen up against oppression and had been martyred fighting in the cause of justice, and that martyrs never die, but are alive and living in the presence of their Maker. These were the most beautiful words that Mālik had heard in the entirety of his short life. Surely somewhere in the heavens far from Earth, his parents could see him. He was afraid that Umm Habīb and Ali would join them and leave him to be on his own. He wanted to be where his loved ones were.

It was early in the morning. Sa'd woke up to the sound of a rooster that was being prepared to be sacrificed by one of the slaves. He yawned and stretched and looked out the window for a moment. Then he suddenly got up and went into the courtyard. He was weary. Fear and apprehension could be seen rushing in waves in his eyes. He looked at their house and at the slaves and maids who worked for them. He went to the stables. About ten young and fresh horses had been tied there. They neighed upon seeing Sa'd. All this wealth was his father's. A father who had ridiculed and humiliated him his whole life for being clumsy or inadequate in some other way, and now, because he had become a petty informant, had found a new respect for him and given him a post of some responsibility and authority in his trade caravan. This is basically what Amr told him last night. And for her part, his mother had become very excited and was no longer worried about him. Sa'd just gazed out and recalled his memories in his mind. Seeing the horses reminded him of the time he defeated Ali badly when they raced each other on horseback. He remembered their playing with their wooden swords and wrestling on the sandy banks of the Euphrates. And ultimately, he remembered the previous day when Ali had rescued him from the clutches of the undercurrents of the Euphrates. He said to himself, "Where would I be right now if it were not for Ali? Where in this land would his wretched corpse have been buried?" These and other kinds of thoughts continued to race through his mind and would not cease. Suddenly he stopped. He took a deep breath and went out.

Ali was calmer than he was the day before. He was sitting under a tree, carving a round-headed doll out of a stick. He was thinking of Samā and how she hugged him. This was the best thing he could come up with to give to her as a memento. Who knows? Perhaps one day when she was grown up, she would give this doll to her children and tell them all about Ali. These thoughts gave Ali courage.

This time, Mālik's mind was chaotic. He was sitting on the riverbank, quietly reciting a melancholy poem. He was not feeling well. Suddenly the sound of a sheep dog caught both their attention. Someone was coming from afar. At first, Ali thought that the dog was barking because of the white goat, who had wanted to get away from the herd twice already this morning, but then he stood up when he saw someone approaching.

It was Sa'd. He was walking slowly, with his head lowered. When Mālik saw that it was Sa'd, he turned to Ali and said, "Its Sa'd... It's Sa'd!"

Ali looked more closely and confirmed that it was indeed Sa'd. Ali thought that he could no longer stand to see him. After their quarrel, it was unlikely that they would be friends again before Ali left.

As a sign that he no longer recognized Sa'd as his friend, Ali went back to where he was sitting and began carving the doll again. But Mālik stood there until Sa'd arrived.

"Salaam alaykum" said S'ad

"Alaykum salaam. What are you doing here?! Have you come to hear what we have to say so that you can go and snitch on us again?" said Malik.

Sa'd looked at Mālik, then said: No, I have come for another purpose. I have come to talk with Ali.

Ali looked at him disdainfully, then said "I have nothing to say to informants. You messed up my plans, so you can rest at east and go home. There's nothing else to report."

Sa'd drew a little closer.

"This time I want to go myself. If you do not go, I will find a way to go myself!"

Ali and Mālik were shocked. Until yesterday, Sa'd considered it a crime to support the grandson of the Prophet, and now he was saying something completely different.

"I want to make up for what I did. My father might be a coward, but I am Sa'd. I am not afraid of anything, not even death."

"You are talking nonsense. You've just come to see if you can make it so we're friends again, but I won't be your friend anymore."

"Fine. But let us bid each other farewell. We might not see each other ever again."

Mālik could not believe his ears. He could not believe that Sa'd was now thinking along the same lines as Ali.

"What made you decide to go?", asked Ali, unable to contain his curiosity.

"I heard that the Umayyads went back on their word and appointed Yazīd [Mu'āwiya's son] as his successor. They say that he is a drunkard and keeps animals as pets; and that he secludes himself in his palace and does not care about the poor. It is a disgrace for such a person to be one's caliph."

"Where did you hear all this from?!"

"The people of the caravan. Yesterday, my father's caravan barely made it to the village."

"What else did they have to say?" asked Ali.

"They said that the grandson of the Prophet refused to pledge allegiance to Yazīd, and that now he was not allowed to continue on to Kūfa and was kept against his will in Nineveh. They also say that Ubaidullah is preparing a large army in Kūfa that might already have arrived."

When Ali heard that Sa'd was saying the same things he had heard his father and Salman say, he accepted Sad's sincerity and said, "Stay and we will go together."

This made Sa'd happy. He walked over to Ali and hugged him. Now Mālik was alone again. He looked at them and then said, "I will come with you too."

Ali and Sa'd were taken by surprise. Ali said, "Are you sure you want to come with us?!"

"You have nothing on me; other than the fact that I am not stubborn like you. Nor do I like competition.

Other than that, my swordsmanship and horsemanship are better than yours."

"So then when do you want to head out?" said Sa'd. "Tomorrow night is when my father and his friends are planning to head out. We must be prepared to leave with them."

"But we are not ready yet!" exclaimed Mālik.

Ali and Sa'd looked at him. Mālik said, "What I mean is food and provisions. I might not be afraid of Ubaidullah's soldiers, but I dread hunger."

Ali and Sa'd laughed out loud, and Mālik joined them. The banks of the Euphrates and the palm trees once again heard the laughter of the boys. Sa'd was happy that he was able to revive a friendship that was in danger of being lost forever.

The sun slowly arose out of the infinite expanse of darkness. The colors of the village came to life out of the darkness, illuminated by its golden rays. Sa'd was waiting behind the wooden door of the house. The sound of a small herd could be heard from the courtyard, and Blacktail, who was waiting impatiently for his friend, clawed at the door. Umm Habīb, who had seen Blacktail's display of his love, said that Blacktail would no longer be a good guardian for the herd; and that he would be leaving for greener pastures of love any day now. She said this, unaware that for his part, Blacktail was plotting to have his female friend join him in his duty of guarding the herd. Finally, Blacktail's claws did their job, and the wooden door opened with a loud creak. Habīb came out of the door with an ashen face and covered his face with a kerchief. His eyes fell on Sa'd, at which moment apprehension could be seen in his big eyes. But he soon recovered and greeted Sa'd, who responded with a hesitance born of shame. Habīb's grandeur always put fear in Sa'd's heart. Despite all of his bad temper, Amr had never been able to equal Habīb's grandeur, and that is why he always hated Habīb and wanted to run him out of everything. Sa'd asked after the boys before Habīb had a chance to say anything. Habīb smiled and limped away. Sa'd looked at him in surprise. What had happened? Had all their plans been thwarted? He was occupied with these thoughts when he heard Ali and Mālik's voices. Blacktail came out of the gate, followed by the herd. Samā was holding the white goat. The boys were surprised to see Sa'd that morning.

"We only have today and tomorrow. We have to practice."

Ali and Mālik looked at each other and affirmed what Sa'd had said. Mālik quickly took all the sheep out of the courtyard. Umm Habīb was looking at them. Seeing Sa'd, she went up to the gate. Mālik's voice had taken over the entire alley. He wanted to finish his job sooner than the previous days no matter what it took, so he grabbed the white goat away from Samā. Every time he took the white goat away from her, he had to do so with the supplications and intercession of Umm Habīb. Mālik's actions increased Umm Habīb's suspicions. After the boys left, she looked out of the door to the courtyard. Something bothered her.

Her eyes were full of sorrow, and a tear was always present in her eyes, ready to run down her cheek. Samā, who had been separated from the white goat again, looked at the herd with greater sorrow than Umm Habīb, and waved to the white goat with her small hands. Umm Habīb shook her head sadly and closed the door.

Habīb was on his way out to the desert and was constantly monitoring his surroundings. Nor did he forget to limp, so that anyone who saw him would have no doubts. The resting place of the large herd was some distance from the village, and the herd was cared for by several shepherds under Habīb's supervision. Inside the village, large stables had been built for the herd, but most of the time the herd was taken out to the desert. Now the desert encampment was under surveillance. Of all the men in the village, Amr was the most eager for Habīb to make the wrong move so that he could hand him over to Sa'd's father and be rid of him forever. One of his men was following Habīb's movements closely. He did so skillfully and in such a way as to evade Habīb's notice. The tracker was fortunate that Habīb went to the desert without a horse, otherwise the sound of his own horse's footsteps would have been heard.

The Euphrates was very calm. The wind created tiny waves on the surface of the water but did so only rarely. The fisherman and his hook were nowhere to be found. The sheep rested around the palm trees. A black horse was tied to a palm tree, and Blacktail and his friend looked from a slight distance at the show the horse's back legs were putting on in trying to break free from the horse's tether. The sound of the boys arguing could be heard from the sand dunes. Mālik was holding a small wooden sword made by Ali, and he was listening to Ali and Sa'd, each of whom gave different directions as to what to do. Mālik was confused, and the horse's endless neighing had his nerves on edge. The fish jumped up and down in the middle of the water and beckoned him to take up his position in his usual battlefield against them. He wasn't sure what to do. After all, the sound of the horse's neighing and the display put on by the fish was better than enduring Sa'd and Ali's contradictory training directions. Ultimately, he threw his wooden sword on the sand and said, "Enough is enough. I'm tired of your bickering. Let one of you teach swordsmanship and let the other act as my opponent. Why have you gone all quiet? What do you have to say for yourselves?"

Ali and Sa'd did not expect such behavior out of Mālik, whom they expected to be grateful for all the techniques that they were teaching him. Ali, who did not want Mālik to be disheartened, thought for a moment and then said, "I will act as your opponent and Sa'd will act as our teacher, and we will then alternate after a while."

Sa'd shrugged his shoulders and said, "That's better. You are very weak. You thrust the sword well, but your grip on it is very weak."

They both had decided to turn Mālik into a brave swordsman and skilled rider in the remaining two days that they had.

Sa'd's father's countless sheep were grazing in the pasture. The shepherds looked after them from afar with the help of sheep dogs, allowing them enough latitude so that they could walk around and graze comfortably. Habīb was coughing hard and continued with his limping. He was also bent over at his waist now and was holding his belly with his hand too. The sound of his moans echoed in the field. There were sheep grazing away for as far as the eye could see. Eventually, Habīb's groaning reached the ear of the shepherds. Two or three of them were frightened and thought that something had happened or that an animal had attacked him. They looked at the dogs and walked towards the encampment. Habīb was lying on the floor with his hand on his stomach. He squeezed his eyes in pain and moaned. He was calling Abdullah, who was the second person in charge of the herd and the shepherds after Habīb himself.

When Abdullah arrived and saw the condition Habīb was in, he quickly took him by his arm and waited for the shepherds to arrive, after which they took him and laid him on a mat in the tent. Abdullah was wondering what had happened to make a man as capable as Habīb moan like this. He thought that perhaps Habīb had been bitten by a snake or stung by a scorpion, and he kept asking questions, which only made Habīb moan more. When the shepherds arrived, they each speculated as to what could be wrong with Habīb, but none had it right. Ultimately it was decided to have Abdullah place Habīb on one of the horses and take him to the village with him. Whatever the matter was, there were more facilities in the village than could be had in the desert, and if something were to happen, they could always send for a doctor to come and see to him, whereas there was nothing to be had in the desert short of some sheep or goat's milk and some wild medicinal herbs. So, everyone agreed with Abdullah.

Amr was making the preparations for a large caravan. He would inventory a list of items left that were in the house's warehouse and kept looking for Sa'd. Bolts of exquisite fabrics, porcelain and crystal vessels, swords, and bejeweled daggers filled the whole warehouse. Amr was told that Sa'd left the house with his horse in the morning and had not returned. He realized that he could not count on him very much. He was berating Sa'd for not taking advantage of this opportunity to be with the new caravan when his informant arrived. He stared at him for a moment, his eyes waiting for any news that he might have.

There was no news. Despite his bad condition, Habīb had made it out to the desert and could not be expected to do anything there. Amr thought for a moment and then said to himself that Habīb must be getting old and no longer had the will and fortitude to fight a war; and that he is perhaps afraid that his brother's fate will befall him too, or that staying in the desert among the sheep has driven the courage out of the warrior and the hero. He grinned and shrugged. He ordered the rest of the villagers to be monitored closely.

The boys were still busy practicing. The sun had passed through its zenith in the sky, which meant that the midday heat had abated somewhat. The sound of the horse's footsteps thrilled Blacktail, who barked at every sound the horse's hooves made. His friend was standing behind one of the palm trees. It was not that he had not seen a horse, but this horse was not any ordinary horse. His neighing could be heard over the entire shoreline of the Euphrates. If the fish could bear to stay out of the water, they too would definitely have come up to sit and watch this unique display of elegance and majesty.

The horse ran at speed, passing through the palm trees, and then returned the way he had gone. The man wanted to control this rebellious creature. A few years ago, Habīb bought the mother of this horse on one of his travels, and he always said that the foals of the horse would make peerless war horses. And it was true. The horse slivered in and out of the palm trees like a snake. Mālik had seen its performance on a couple of occasions. Most of the time, Sa'd used ordinary horses from the stables for equestrian training, but this time he preferred to bring out his best horse because of the importance of the training. He brought out the horse that every warrior dreamed of owning. Sa'd finished his practice run, and now it was Ali's turn, after which it was Mālik who had to ride the horse again after a long absence. As soon as Ali got on the horse, it rose on its two hind legs and let out a loud neighing sound. Mālik closed his eyes for fear of seeing something he did not want to see. When he opened his eyes again, he expected to see Ali lying on the ground, and if God was with him, he would be spared from being trampled under the horse's hooves. But the horse calmed down very quickly and resumed the exercise of running among the palm trees. Mālik slowly opened his eyes. He was pale with fear. Ali rode the horse in a serpentine pattern between the palms, twirling his sword over his head and hitting the sticks he had placed in the palms to represent his opponents. Sa'd applauded him involuntarily. Mālik wondered if he could ride this rebellious animal at all. If he was even able to ride it, he would surely find enough time to think about striking the wooden figures with his sword as well.

Abdullah had placed Habīb on a horse face down and had taken the reins and was leading the horse on foot until they reached the village. It seems he knew about Habīb's secret plans.

"What good would my staying in the village do? You have Ali and Mālik, and I do not have anyone."

"Do not insist."

"Is the issue one of being true to one's religion?"

"You know what the issue is. You have to pay off your debt first, and only then…"

Abdullah thought for a moment and stopped moving. The horse stopped with him. Habīb raised his head and looked at Abdullah.

"What's going on?? You want someone to see you and become suspicious? Come on, get a move on. Let's go!"

Abdullah pulled at the reins and started to move again.

"Don't worry. Nobody's here. Can I come with you if I pay off my debt?"

"Don't talk so much. And where will you get all this money from?"

"I have a precious ring that is a memento from my mother. I had kept it for a day when I could sell it to buy a herd of sheep after I had paid off my debt."

"Who are you going to sell it to? The creditor that I know will not be satisfied with anything but cash money."

The village was gradually coming into view. Habīb raised his head and saw the village.

"If he does not accept the ring, do not be stubborn and insist. Too bad you hadn't thought of selling the ring sooner and come out from under the burden of the interest on your loan."

"If I succeed in selling it, how can I join up with you?"

"We will leave tomorrow night. We will meet up outside the village between the palm trees."

"So this putting on a show of being ill will continue until tomorrow, will it?"

Abdullah laughed and shook his head. Habīb gritted his teeth angrily. Perhaps he regretted trusting him. But he had known Abdullah for years; ever since his father was killed on the way with Habīb's caravan and his family had been left homeless. When Abdullah grew up, he wanted to provide capital for his own people and start a trade caravan of his own instead of working for someone else. That was how he had entered into debt and was later selected to work as a shepherd through Habīb's mediation. Now he was paying half of what he was earning to service his debt, and he wished he could one day get out from under the burden of the bad mistake that he had made. It was a simple error, but his stubbornness always got him in trouble. But whatever the case might be, he could be trusted to keep his mouth shut, which is why Habīb had told him of his plans to leave, despite the show that he was putting on for everyone else's benefit.

***

The boys shouted out to Mālik. He had fallen to the ground and the horse stood next to him and was watching him. His whole body was covered in dust. He was lucky to have fallen on some soft sand. Ali was very concerned for Mālik's arms and legs, which he moved around to see if there were any fractures. Mālik wanted to say something but his mouth was covered with dust, and he could not get a word out. Ali thought he had lost his ability to speak and became very scared. Mālik coughed and slowly spit the dust out of his mouth. Sa'd slapped him hard on his back.

"Is it not possible for a soldier not to ride a horse? Being an infantryman is better for me."

He got up with difficulty and walked towards the river. He patted down all the dust from his head and body with his hand. Sa'd and Ali looked at each other.

"Are you sure he can come with us?!" asked S'ad.

"Not all soldiers need to be on horseback!"

He then got up and looked at Mālik, who was sitting by the water, washing his head and face.

"That's enough for today. We will practice some more tomorrow."

"I'll come a little later. Someone might get suspicious."

Mālik was still coughing and pouring water on his head and face so as to leave no trace of any dust or dirt on him, oblivious of his white shirt, which now looked to be anything but white!

Abdullah came out of Sa'd's house. He had a big smile on his face, and he was tossing a small purse of money up and down in his hand.

"Well, I tricked them but good! If he knew what my intentions were, he would have strangled me with his own hands," said Abdullah to himself.

These were the kinds of things that he said as he left.

It was night, and the sky was filled with millions of stars. But the moon was nowhere to be found. Whenever the moon was out, it illuminated everything with its light. But now it was dark, and nothing could be seen. A light came on in one of the village courtyards. It was Habīb's house. Ali and Mālik had woken up in the middle of the night and were doing things covertly. Ali took six loaves of bread and a few dates and put them in a bundle. Mālik stood above him holding three large fish.

"What are these for?! What we have here is enough! The caravan is not far from our village. We'll be able to reach them soon."

"We might have to hide somewhere for a while because of the Kūfan soldiers. We must have enough provisions!"

Mālik was so insistent that Ali agreed to put the fish in the bundle as well. Then the two of them put the bundle in a corner of the yard in an earthenware jar that was surrounded by flowers. It was the last night they were going to be at home, and they wanted to enjoy the village at night. Mālik thought of his sisters and Umm Habīb, and Ali thought of Samā and the wooden doll that was the only thing he could give her to remember him by.

Umm Habīb stayed up all night like a child. She could not sleep. She had somehow caught on to the fact that Habīb and the boys were hiding something from her, but she did not know what it was. At the same time, she prayed for the grandson of the Prophet with tears in her eyes. She was crying for the fact that she was in a village that was close to where the grandson of the Prophet was, but that she was still not able to go and see him.

Habīb was staring at the ceiling in the darkness of the room, thinking of the plan he had made. When he came in from the desert, Salman had come to treat him, and that is when all the appointments had been arranged. He had told them that Abdullah might join them among the palm trees outside the village. All the i's were dotted and the t's crossed. All the preparations had been made for them to join the Imam's caravan. The soldiers were unable to see them under cover of the darkness of the night. Habīb knew the way and had many years of experience as a scout. He knew when to move so that no creature would notice any motion. During those nights, none of the villagers could sleep, not even Sa'd's father. Everyone knew that the Prophet's grandson was besieged by Yazīd's forces near their village. Imam Husain's ﷺ caravan was besieged somewhere not far from them, but in circumstances that made going there even more difficult than a long-distant pilgrimage to Mecca. Everyone wanted to make this pilgrimage in their heart of hearts, but the fear of doing so could be seen on their faces. Fear of Ibn Ziād who had become the governor of Kūfa, and against whom no one dared to rise up. Every single one of the villagers hated Yazīd and Ibn Ziād in their heart of hearts. Many had heard the story of the justice and righteous behavior of Ali ibn Abī Tālib ﷺ and his sons. Like all people who hated injustice, they too wished to destroy Yazīd, but they had grown so afraid of the government that they listened to Sa'd's father and crawled into a corner of their respective houses. Some were even afraid to think these thoughts in the privacy of their own minds! Political oppression was rife everywhere, even in a small village that was a long way away from Kūfa.

Meanwhile, Abdullah had become sleepless in the desert. He sat under the light of the stars and constantly counted and recounted the money in the purse and happily put it back in the purse. It was a difficult night. At times, it seemed as if the sun had no intention of ever showing herself again.

Morning finally arrived and a commotion spread throughout the village. The people's longing to help the Prophet's grandson who was besieged by Yazīd's forces not too far from their village was nowhere to be seen or heard. It seemed they preferred to forget that the leader of the House of the Prophet, a man who was famous for the soundness of his character and for the purity of his soul, was surrounded with his whole family and retinue a few miles away, and everyone feared that the great armies of Kūfa and Damascus would massacre them all at any given moment.

There was a great commotion in the hearts of the boys. It was the last day that the Euphrates saw them. It was not clear whether they would be able to return and play along the banks of the Euphrates and among the palm trees, blissfully unaware of the troubles of the world around them. Mālik was still afraid of riding on horseback and wanted to join the army as "an infantryman", as he said. Saʿd drew his sword with greater force and helped Mālik deliver his blows with greater force on his opponent. The white goat had become ill. When morning came, tears welled up in Umm Habīb and Samā's eyes, and it was perhaps on account of the boys that the white goat was grief-stricken and gazed at the palm trees and his usual escape route.

Habīb was lying in bed at home. He was intent on continuing to play the same role for Umm Habīb and his wife until nightfall. Umm Habīb entered the room with a large cloth in her hand. Habīb started moaning and groaning, but as soon as he did so, Umm Habīb grinned and said, "Don't playact for me! Here, I brought this for you."

She placed the cloth on the floor next to Habīb's bed. Habīb looked at her in shock at having been found out. His last moan dried up in his mouth. Umm Habīb's wrinkled and trembling hands opened the cloth. It contained a large sword that had a very sharp edge. Habīb got up from his reclining position involuntarily and sat straight up.

"What's this?!"

"I know all about your plans. This is my gift. I want you to defend the justice and purity of the Family of the Prophet with this sword."

Tears welled up in Habīb's eyes. He involuntarily threw himself into his mother's arms like a child.

"This is the only thing left of your father's. He used it in the Battle of Nahrawān."

By now Habīb was crying out loud.

"Calm down. You are a brave warrior. I wish I too was able to hold a sword in my hand!"

Umm Habīb comforted him and caressed his hair with her hand. Although she was barely able to control her emotions and gently wiped the tears from her own cheeks, she firmly encouraged Habīb. And this made it much easier for Habīb to leave.

Night had fallen and Ali and Mālik picked up their bundle and left the house before Habīb and his friends left. They used Sa'd as their pretext so that no one would suspect them.

They were waiting in the alley for their father to come out. Sa'd was supposed to wait for them at the end of the village road. Mālik had taken out a loaf of bread and was eating it slowly. He said that eating made him forget about his anxieties. Finally, Habīb came out and the boys followed him covertly, being sure to maintain a great distance between them. Salman was supposed to join Habīb and his friends, followed by two others from the village. It was dark everywhere and only the light of the stars shone a little light on the earth. Salman was there, at the appointed time and place, and then the two others and, as Habīb had said, Abdullah also joined them outside the village. Nothing could be heard except the barking of dogs and the chirping of crickets. Habīb and his friends walked slowly, and the boys followed them even more slowly. As they went forward, suddenly a few people fell upon them and surprised them. Then Amr showed up. Habīb wanted to draw his sword, but they were so surprised that they could not do anything.

"So now you have taken to acting ill in order to deceive us, ey?" growled Amr.

He grabbed Habīb by his hair angrily.

The boys looked around anxiously. They were worried about Sa'd. Things would get worse if he showed himself.

Amr's voice could be heard singing a battle song loudly. Mālik was terrified and could not eat the rest of his bread. Habīb was silent and did not say anything.

"Don't you want to know who ruined your plans?! What kind of scout are you?? What kind of leader of Kūfa caravans are you now, with all those years of experience of yours not coming to your aid?"

It was as if he was taking out all his years of frustration by giving expression to these thoughts. Salman wanted to respond to him in kind, but Habīb calmed him down by making a sign with one of his hands.

"Why lie?! The show you put on certainly deceived us, and it was a good plan that would have enabled you to reach the caravan of Husain ibn Ali.

But this time you were fooled by a child, with all that experience of yours. Truly, I am surprised by you."

Habīb looked around for a moment with questioning eyes. Now his hands had been tied tightly with rope, and he could not move. Abdullah's voice constantly kept repeating in his mind.

It must have been him. No one knew about it except for him and a few others.

Habīb was deep in the midst of these thoughts when he was completely taken aback by Sa'd who appeared and stood next to Amr. Everyone was looking on in surprise and disbelief.

Ali and Mālik too were looking with eyes wide open in

disbelief at a scene that they could not take in. All this time, Sa'd had been playing them along in order to find out Habīb's plan and departure time.

Silence had taken over everywhere. Amr's men peacefully took Habīb and his friends to Sa'd's house in the dark of night.

It was unclear what they intended to do with them. The boys were frozen in place, like a couple of scarecrows. Sa'd had appeared exactly at the appointed time, not to join them, but to betray them.

Ali was so angry that it was as if blood had covered his eyes. He wanted to attack Sa'd, but Mālik grabbed his hands with some difficulty and kept him at bay until Sa'd and Amr left with the prisoners they had taken.

Abdullah was sitting among the palm trees, waiting. He had a sword and some food with him. He constantly looked in the direction of the village from behind the palms to see when Habīb and his friends would join him.

Morning was breaking. Ali and Mālik were sitting in the courtyard with their bundle of provisions, tired and frustrated. They talked about Saʿd and the big trick that he had played on them. They talked and talked; there was no end to all they had to talk about. No one could believe that Saʿd could be so deceitful and cunning and could trick Ali so easily.

"But Saʿd was *with* us. He even brought his horse. His *best* horse!!" said Ali with frustration in his voice.

And to think that Saʿd had done this to Ali, who was his best friend, and who had saved him from certain death. For a moment, Ali thought to himself that he wished he had not saved him from the waves of the river that day and that Saʿd had not survived and lived to be able to stab him in the back with such a poisonous dagger. A thought came to Mālik again, and he said that maybe pressure had been applied to Sa'd to betray them. "But who knew that we were up to something anyway?"

All of the speculation and ifs and buts and maybes came and went from Mālik's mind and kept on repeating themselves in circles. The teenage warriors who thought they had drawn a brilliant plan and could easily join Imam Husain's ﷺ caravan were now like a defeated army who could not believe that they had taken a spy and a traitor into their midst and accepted him as a friend.

Ali kept slapping one of his hands with his other hand and Mālik kept slapping his own forehead, wondering why they had been duped into trusting Sa'd *again*, after he had informed on them once already. If they had not accepted him back that day, they would not be in this situation now, and would have reached the caravan by now.

The situation was the exact opposite in Sa'd's house. Sa'd's father had positioned him next to himself and put his arm around his neck. A strange kind of passion could be seen in his face.

"I am so proud of you! Not anyone could have pulled this off you know!!"

Sa'd had an artificial smile at the corner of his mouth. Although he could not have dream of all this love and attention and praise, his conscience tormented him and would not give him peace. He knew full well what thoughts were going through Ali's and Mālik's minds now. And they had every right to be thinking such thoughts. Even one's enemy doesn't stab his opponent in the back like that. Amr was happier than everyone else. He said, "My own stupid people did not even suspect Habīb."

He applauded Sa'd and cheered him on. He said that Sa'd was now capable of managing a battalion of professional soldiers, let alone a small commercial convoy. These words of praise made his father even happier. He did not want the villagers to worry unduly. That is why he wanted to keep Habīb and his friends in the desert in tents temporarily until the whole incident with the Prophet's grandson blew over, after which everything would be forgotten, and they could then be released. That was the best thing that could be done. After all, Habīb was highly respected by the villagers and had close ties to many of them. Everyone knew that Sa'd's father was respected only because of his large herds and wealth, but Habīb was honored by everyone for his honesty and righteous behavior.

But Amr was of a different opinion. He said, "Leave them to me. I will do something to make holding onto them worth more than a thousand bolts of fine silk and tens of thousands of boxes of gold and jewelry."

He said that he had many plans with which he could make Sa'd's father endeared to the Umayyad government with just these few prisoners. Sa'd was afraid of Amr's words. He was thinking, "What did he want to do with the prisoners?"

Habīb and Salman and their friends were sitting with their hands and feet tied on the floor of the house's cellar among all the valuables that were packaged and neatly stacked on top of each other. They were so shocked that they had forgotten to talk. Light came in through a wooden-framed window and signaled the arrival of morning. Habīb was constantly searching his mind. Where had his plans gone wrong? He had not told his plans to anyone. Except for Umm Habīb and his friends that joined him, and… Abdullah. Abdullah, Abdullah, Abdullah. This name did not leave his mind alone, even for a moment. If he had not disclosed the plan to anyone, then how did Sa'd come to know of it? Abdullah must have sold his ring to none other than Sa'd. But what use did Sa'd have for such a ring? That is, why did Sa'd have to do what he did to Ali, after Ali had saved his life?? Was he not friends with the boys? Salman had started a coughing fit. One of Habīb's friends was asleep, and the other had his head on his knees.

Salman said to Habīb "Look where we ended up instead of with Imam Husain's caravan? Who do you think could have informed on us to this tyrant?"

"I don't know. I'm confused. Nobody knows where we are, so that they could at least do something to save us. Poor Umm Habīb. She thinks that by now we have joined up with the forces of her master Imam Husain."

"Umm Habīb? Does she know?"

"She cottoned on. She bid me farewell with her own hands."

It was a difficult day. These thoughts were running through the minds of each and every one of them. Everyone was looking to find out what the truth of the matter was, unaware that there was another group in the village who wanted to follow them and join the caravan. The light gradually made its way through the wooden-framed windows of the cellar. Amr was standing behind the window, staring at Habīb. He felt victorious. It was not clear what fate awaited the prisoners.

The village could be seen from a distance. Abdullah had fallen asleep among the palm trees. Mosquitoes swirled around his head, and he could hear the sound of stray dogs. He opened his eyes slowly. The light bothered him. He rubbed his eyes gently with his hands. He had waited until morning, then fell asleep where he was, unaware of what had happened to Habīb and his friends. He was anxious. He looked around. He thought they had forgotten him and gone the other way. He got up and went back to the village.

All the alleys of the village were deserted, except for the stray dogs that roamed the streets. The wooden door of the house was closed. Ali and Mālik were asleep in the middle of the courtyard with their food bundle next to them. Umm Habīb looked at the boys and then at the stable. With trembling hands, she picked up the bundle and inspected its contents: fish, bread, and dates. She was surprised. There were two swords lying next to their clothes. Now she was able to put it all together. Why were the boys sleeping here with swords and a bundle of food? She put her hand on Ali's shoulder and called his name. Ali shifted slightly and half-opened his eyes. He was a little shocked to see Umm Habīb. But the sound of the knocking at the front door raised Umm Habīb's attention. They were knocking on the door with heavy blows. Ali quickly woke Mālik up, but when his eyes fell on the food bundle and the swords, the color faded from his face. Now everything was going to come out. Umm Habīb opened the door. Abdullah was standing behind the door. He asked about Habīb's whereabouts sleepily and lethargically. When he heard that he was not home, he became convinced that he had been left behind.

"Where is he? They left without me!"

Abdullah and Umm Habīb's voices could be heard from the door. Ali realized that Abdullah had planned to leave too. Mālik slowly opened his eyes. His whole body was cramped. Ali got up and stood quietly at the door. Abdullah entered and sat in the middle of the courtyard.

"I will stay here until he comes back and takes me."

Umm Habīb was looking at the boys to see what was going on, but they didn't understand what Abdullah was saying either.

"I sold my ring and gave Amr the money I owed him. What other obligation did I have that prevented me from joining them?"

He was saying these things in a plaintiff manner. Gradually Umm Habīb started to become worried. Habīb was not one to deceive someone and not keep his promise. Something must have happened. "What business did you have with Habīb?"

The boys looked at Umm Habīb with concern on their faces. Abdullah wiped his tears with the back of his sleeve.

"You did not know. Habīb and some men from the village were planning on going to help Husain ibn Ali."

"And you were supposed to go with them?"

Now Umm Habīb's face had turned red. Her voice trembled like her hands. Ali and Mālik also looked at each other with concern.

"They left last night, but my son was never one not to keep his promises."

She said this and then looked worriedly at Ali and Mālik. They were speechless from the fear they felt inside. They did not know what to say, as their plans had been exposed to Umm Habīb by the food bundle and their swords.

"Why did you two come back? Weren't you planning on leaving too??"

Ali tried to reply, "Yes, but…"

Umm Habīb approached Ali with trembling legs. She put her hand on Ali's shoulders. Staring into Ali's eyes, she wanted to make him speak.

"Tell me ... why did you come back?!"

"Amr and his men were lying in wait. They arrested them and took them away!"

"You mean someone knew of their plans?" asked Abdullah in disbelief.

"Yes. Sa'd revealed our plan and ambushed us." said Mālik:

Umm Habīb hit herself on the head with both her hands.

"They were taken to Sa'd's house. We have to do something!" said Ali.

Habīb and his friends were placed on horses with their hands and feet tied. They covered their mouths and eyes with handkerchiefs so that they could not see anything and so they could not make any sound. Habīb tried to get out of his blindfold and the handkerchief that was placed on his mouth. But Amr was watching what Habīb was doing. He told him,

"I will do something to you to make sure you'll leave this village forever!"

They mounted the last person onto one of the horses. Amr told them, "Take a route where no one can see where you are going. I don't want anyone to know where you are taking them."

Sa'd was standing in a corner of the courtyard, looking at Amr and the prisoners in surprise.

Ali was standing in the alley with Mālik and Abdullah, thinking of a way to find out about what was happening to Habīb and his friends. Ali thought that if he ever saw Sa'd, he would pummel him to a pulp. Mālik thought that if Umm Habīb interceded with Sa'd's father, he might be prevailed upon to release the prisoners.

Abdullah couldn't think of anything useful to do. He was so afraid of Sa'd's father and of Amr that he was unable to do anything. The wooden door opened, letting out Amr's men and the prisoners one at a time. One could not identify any of the prisoners. Ali counted: One, two, three, four. He was counting the prisoners on horseback who had had their eyes and mouths covered with kerchiefs. Their number equaled the number of people who were arrested the night before.

Ali whispered, "That's all four of them. Where are they taking them, I wonder?"

"We must follow them." said Abdullah,

"But we don't have any horses."

This is where Abdullah's fast legs came into play. He ran so fast in the desert between the encampments to deliver food and news to the shepherds that he often outpaced the war horses. Ali and Mālik were surprised to see that he wanted to chase the horses. But when the gate was closed and the horses started walking, Abdullah quickly followed them with his thin, fast legs, leaving the boys behind in the alley. They hesitated, but then Ali decided to follow Abdullah.

———————◆———————

Sa'd's father was livid. Sa'd was standing next to him. His father said, "What else have you done without my knowledge? Don't you know that if the villagers found out, they would make this village a living hell for me?"

Amr was standing in a corner, keeping his cool.

"That's why I had them sent out to the desert. If the villagers got a hint of what had taken place and came over here to investigate, they would not find anyone here."

Sa'd's father, who still did not understand what Amr had been up to, asked more angrily, "Let them stay right there. I will release them when the dispute between Yazīd and Husain ibn Ali blows over."

"This is the best opportunity. You have to offer up the prisoners."

"Offer up the prisoners to whom??"

Amr's words did not sit well with Sa'd at all. He had gone pale and was afraid they would be harmed. If this happened, his friends would never forget his betrayal for as long as they lived. And Sa'd might not be able ever to escape this torment of his conscience either.

Amr continued, "To Umar bin Sa'd, of course. He and an army of Kūfan warriors have arrayed their tents before Husain ibn Ali and his retinue. He can make him surrender in a day. We should not miss this opportunity."

"I am not interested in war. I do not want to lose Habīb."

"By doing so, you can become one of the government's allies. If you hand over the prisoners, you will be able to gain concessions from the government in their stead."

Sa'd's father ran a hand over his beard. In that moment, Sa'd came to hate Amr. How could anyone be so hard-hearted? But when he remembered what he had done himself, he realized that he himself was the main cause of bringing about this situation. He shook his head in despair and left.

Ali and Mālik ran panting after Abdullah, who had put a long distance between them and himself. This was the only way they could find out where Habīb and the others were being taken. After a while, Abdullah returned at speed. He was shouting loudly, but it was unclear what it was that he was saying. The closer he got, the clearer his words became.

"Go back! Go back!!"

The boys were confused. They hesitated for a bit and then started to turn back. They did not return with any enthusiasm, but they felt that something had happened to make Abdullah tell them to go back. They ran until they reached the palm trees near the village, at which point they both threw themselves on the ground and collapsed like corpses. The palm trees offered good cover and a good place to hide. If anyone was following Abdullah, they could not see them anymore. As soon as they recovered their breath, Abdullah arrived. He was out of breath too. Sweat ran down from his forehead and his lips were dry.

"It worked out for the best." he said, breathlessly.

Ali and Mālik were waiting to see what had happened.

"It all worked out for the best. Nobody knows that I wanted to go with them."

The boys did not understand what he was saying.

"They were taken to the encampment. I can go back there easily and release them when the time is right."

Now Ali and Mālik understood what Abdullah meant. No one knew that Abdullah wanted to go with them. After Habīb, he was the second shepherd in charge of the herd. He could easily go back there and get to them. Perhaps if Amr did not go through with his plan to hand them over to Umar ibn Sa'd, they would be able to release them.

***

Sa'd came out of the village on horseback together with Amr and his father. The black horse was riding at a gallop again. Sa'd, who had prevented Ali from joining the caravan of the Prophet's grandson with his treachery, was now travelling on the road with his father and Amr in the direction that Ali was supposed to have taken the previous night.

They gradually passed by the palm trees and started to gallop along the bank of the Euphrates. The farther they went, the wider the desert became, where no trees or bushes were to be seen. It was the Nineveh desert. The tents could be seen from afar. A caravan with a few tents could be seen to one side, and a large caravan with countless tents was on the other.

Amr declared, "As you can see, this is the Desert of the Gathering (*mahshar*).[3] It is clear who is going to win this war."

"The Prophet's grandson should not have come here. He should have pledged allegiance to Yazīd and saved himself all this trouble."

Sa'd was calm. He was looking at the throng of tents. He had never seen such a scene before.

When they climbed down from the horses, everywhere was teeming with people. They were told that the main army had not yet arrived and that Umar ibn Sa'd wanted to end this affair peacefully by convincing the grandson of the Prophet to pledge allegiance to Yazīd. Amr talked with a few people. Sa'd's father, who as usual was wearing expensive clothing, had lowered his head among the crowd and did not want to talk to anyone. Sa'd looked around with great curiosity. If he truly wanted to join forces with Husain ibn Ali ﷺ, he could have gotten

---

[3] Reference to the Gathering on the Day of Resurrection. – Translator.

there very easily from where he was. But then he thought that he would surely be stopped by some of Amr's men, and if he was very clever and was able to get by them, then he would surely face the greater barrier of Omar ibn Sa'd's soldiers. He was deep in these thoughts when Amr decided to go after a certain man. There was a large tent among the multitude of tents, and it was clear that it was a special tent. When he got there, he was told to wait outside the tent. Sounds from inside the tent could be heard clearly. Inside the tent, Qarāh ibn Sufyān al-Hanżali was talking to Umar ibn Sa'd. He was providing a report of his negotiations with Husain ibn Ali ﷺ. Umar bin Sa'd listened intently to hear the position of the Prophet's grandson. Now Sa'd's ears were paying full attention.

"Husain ibn Ali said to tell him on his behalf that the people of this city wrote a letter to him and told him that they had no leader and asked him to come to them; and he trusted them but they deceived him, even though eighteen thousand of them had pledged their allegiance to him. When he got close [to Kūfa] and became aware of their deception, he wanted to go back to where he came from, but Hurr ibn Yazīd prevented him from doing so, forcing him to decamp here. Husain ibn Ali ﷺ said that you and he have close family ties and asked to be free to return to whence he came based on those ties of kinship."

These were the words that Husain ibn Ali ﷺ relayed to Umar ibn Sa'd in response to his demand that he pledges allegiance to Yazīd. This time, the breaking of covenants was on a higher level. It was something that disturbed Sa'd greatly every time he heard about it, thanks to his evil act of treachery. He remembered the covenant of friendship he had made with Ali and Mālik years ago; the night that he had broken the whole covenant and betrayed his best friend in order to garner his father's favor and in order to gain worldly wealth.

Umar bin Sa'd was confused. He ordered a letter to be written to Ibn Ziād in which the Imam's reply was to be stated. He hoped that Ibn Ziād would exempt him and his soldiers from confronting the Prophet's grandson. Even Umar ibn Sa'd did not want to draw a sword on the grandson of the Prophet, a man whose father and brother, like himself, were as famous for their righteousness and code of moral conduct as they were for their sense of justice. Husain ibn Ali's ﷺ words had made Sa'd's father concerned, and he looked at the tents with anxiety. His hands and feet were reluctant to enter the tent of Umar bin Sa'd.

Sa'd's father exclaimed, "The Devil be damned! This uprising would not have started if Mu'āwiya had kept the promise he gave to Hasan ibn Ali and had not appointed Yazīd as his successor, thereby inaugurating a hereditary kingship in the caliphate."

Amr retorted, "Don't tell me you want to go to the tents on the other side? And to stand against the will of the government??"

When Sa'd's father heard Amr speak these words, he quickly came back to himself, and they entered the tent, offering their salaams. Sa'd followed them into the tent. Now Sa'd was becoming more and more aware of Ali's words to the effect that his father was a coward, and that he preferred his own interests and worldly wealth to that which was right. Umar bin Sa'd was seated inside the tent. He asked for their names, and Amr responded in an obsequious manner. Umar bin Sa'd paid no attention to them until the names of the prisoners were mentioned, at which point he asked about the number of prisoners and the distance to their village. Amr answered each question carefully and in turn. Sa'd's father was silent. He preferred to leave everything to Amr.

"There are four prisoners… No, there are no others… They are being kept in an encampment outside the village."

Finally, they left the tent after kissing Umar bin Sa'd hand and taking his orders, which were to keep the prisoners safe and to be vigilant so as to ensure that no one would join up with Husain ibn Ali ﷺ.

Now Sa'd felt somewhat better. After all, keeping Habīb in an encampment in the desert was much more preferable than sending him to Kūfa where he would be thrown in a dark hole in the ground which passed as a prison. Whenever his brother described the prisons of Kūfa and the Levant, and the fate of the unfortunate prisoners that were kept there, Sa'd's hands trembled.

Umm Habīb had decided to go to Saʿd's father and ask him to release his son. By now everyone knew what had happened to Habīb. Samā was acting up. Ali and Mālik were looking for a way to help Abdullah. Everything was in disarray. In the meantime, Amr was acting like the most important person in the village, watching the village like a hawk so that no one could move a muscle without his being aware of it. News of everyone's comings and goings were reported to Amr without fail, which is why the boys couldn't go anywhere easily without being reported.

In the meantime, Abdullah had managed to make his way out to the desert and was busy trying to implement his plans. Amr's people were watching Habīb and the others in the main encampment. In addition to overseeing the largest herd and shepherds who were at the main encampment, Abdullah kept a keen vigil over Amr's agents. He had not yet been able to spot Habīb. Meanwhile, Abdullah's presence there had turned Habīb's suspicions about him into certainty. Unaware of everything, Abdullah had been transformed into a great traitor in Habīb's mind; into someone who had attained much by snitching on others. When the guards called out to Abdullah, it was all Habīb could do to prevent himself from exploding. He said that if he was ever released, he would teach him a lesson he would not forget about why one should not betray one's friends. For his part, Abdullah was waiting for an opportunity, no matter how brief, to talk to Habīb and tell him what was really going on.

Now the news had spread among the villagers as well, thanks to Amr leaking it. By doing so, he hoped to dampen the effect of Habīb's courage and heroism among the people and instilled fear in the hearts of the villagers so that no one else would dare make a move.

The boys were finally able to prevail upon Umm Habīb. They wanted to try their luck first, and appeal to Sa'd's father only if and after they did not succeed. Mālik planned to go to the desert to obtain news of Habīb from Abdullah. But Ali said that Sa'd had revealed his father's plans and that Amr, and his agents now knew that they were aware of everything, so that Mālik's plan would only endanger Abdullah and ruin everything else. Ali was constantly walking back and forth, thinking. The sound of the sheep who wanted to go out was driving him crazy. Although Umm Habīb and Ali's mother had milked the herd, they still craved their daily routine of freely grazing outdoors and being able to walk along the riverbank, and this made them pine to get out of the narrow confines of the barn. Blacktail was the most impatient of them all. He wanted to jump over the wall and go and play with his friend. Finally, despite all the noise and pressure that was on him, Ali came up with an idea.

He asked Umm Habīb to give him some medicinal herbs that would put people to sleep. Mālik realized what Ali was thinking. He could have put Amr's agents to sleep merely by delivering the sleeping medicine to Abdullah, after which he could easily free his father and the three other prisoners. Umm Habīb quickly went over to her small medicine cabinet and returned with a packet of medicine that was in a small cloth-covered jar. Ali asked Umm Habīb to act like she had gone mad and to go out to the desert and ask Abdullah about Habīb. That was the only thing they could do. Perhaps Amr's agents would not bother the old woman who had, after all, lost both of her sons and had now ostensibly gone out of her mind.

The boys brought Umm Habīb's robe. She hid the bottle of the medicinal herbs in the folds of her clothes and headed out. Every villager who saw Umm Habīb in her miserable state felt sorry for her and went up to her and comforted her. Umm Habīb in turn asked them about what had happened to Habīb. She played her role so well that Ali and Mālik, who were walking behind her, came to believe that Umm Habīb, unaware of everything, had really gone mad because of Habīb's absence. Neighbors who saw Habīb's pitiful state could not stop their tears from running down their cheeks.

"May God curse them. Look what they have done to this old woman!"

"Poor old woman. There is a limit to how much sorrow and grief one can endure!"

Now Umm Habīb was no longer playing a role. She had never been able to cry so easily and peacefully during the years since Mālik's father's death. She was now crying and wailing for real and heading out of the village into the desert. Amr's soldiers blocked her way when she reached the palm trees. Umm Habīb begged them to help her find her son. She said that maybe a wolf had attacked the herd and killed Habīb, and that all she wanted to do was to go and find his bloody clothes. The boys were worried. They prayed that Umm Habīb would be able to pass Amr's agents and reach the main encampment. No matter how many times Amr's agents said that Habīb was alive but that he was a prisoner, it made no difference to Umm Habīb, who just kept repeating herself like a madwoman. Eventually they had had enough of her madness and let her pass just so they would be rid of her nuisance. The boys secretly jumped for joy, as perhaps the biggest step in their plan had now met with success. Umm Habīb made her way slowly towards the camp. She became tired and sat down for a while to catch her breath, then started walking again. Abdullah spotted her when she reached the encampment. He told Amr's agents that she was Habīb's mother. They wanted to arrest her and take her back to the village. Abdullah prayed to God to allow him to reach Umm Habīb. He said in a loud voice that Habīb was not there, and that she should return to the village. For her part, Umm Habīb pretended not to hear what Abdullah said and kept calling out for Habīb in her crazy way.

Habīb heard his mother's familiar voice. But he could not shout out to her as they had covered the prisoners' mouths with kerchiefs so that their voices would not be heard. Whenever their mouths were opened so that they could take in some food, Habīb would start shouting. It was the only way for him to let the shepherds know that they were imprisoned there.

Abdullah finally reached Umm Habīb, and then asked, "Why are you here? The men have been imprisoned. They will not let me go near them."

Umm Habīb had tears in her eyes, and her lips were dry. Abdullah, who saw her condition, sat her on a rock and left her to herself temporarily to go and get some water. Umm Habīb looked around. The presence of her son there was soothing. The fat sheep were busy grazing as far as the eye could see, their udders bursting with milk.

Abdullah returned with a bowl of water. Umm Habīb gently lifted the bowl, put it to her mouth, and drained it. She then said, "I have brought you something with which you can put these no-good rascals to sleep and save my son and the others."

Abdullah's eyes widened in surprise. Umm Habīb quickly gave him the bottle of medicinal herbs and Abdullah hid it in the folds of his clothes.

"I will certainly try my best."

"Tell them the old woman has gone crazy and has come to look for her son. Say that you convinced her that he was not here and that he had taken ill and returned home."

Abdullah nodded his agreement. When she finished what she had to say, she got up and started walking back to the village.

Amr's agents interrogated Abdullah, "Why had she come? What did she say? Watch out for her guile!"

Abdullah assured them that he was more concerned than they were that the prisoners would not get away. Hearing these words made Habīb even more suspicious of Abdullah.

Now everything depended on Abdullah. He was going to try to mix the sleeping medicine into the officers' food at the first chance he got.

Sa'd had nothing to do during this time. He always used to spend his days playing and competing with Ali. Now he had nothing to make him happy and no friend with whom he could talk or compete against. He was left on his own. Amr, who was aware that Sa'd's conscience was tormenting him, tried to burden him with the responsibility of some important tasks as a distraction. So, he had put him in charge of his informers, and any news that was brought to him was reported to him through Sa'd. Of course, Amr was much smarter than that. It was really just a show to allow him to keep Sa'd close by so that he could watch over him personally.

The night sky was full of bright stars. Ali wished he had never had a friend named Sa'd. But it was too late for that now. Now all he had left was his regret. If Abdullah succeeded to free his father, they might be able to reach the Prophet's grandson's army again by some other route. Mālik was thinking the same thoughts. Blacktail's friend had become concerned about her friend's absence and had come over to the village to see what the problem was. She scratched at the door with her paws and barked. Blacktail was struggling from behind the door to open it and see his friend.

"I will take the sheep out tomorrow." said Ali,

"Nothing is certain yet. Maybe we can try to leave again tomorrow." replied Mālik.

"Taking the sheep out will be a good excuse for us to find out what is happening outside the house."

The shepherds took turns guarding the herd, and the dogs were more vigilant than they were during the day. Abdullah could not sleep. He wanted to go to see Habīb several times, but each time he approached the main encampment, he saw Amr's agents sitting around the fire talking. It was as if they were not affected by sleep. Abdullah stared into the distance, perhaps in the direction where the tents of Husain ibn Ali ﷺ and his entourage had been set up. He wished he could get to them with his fast legs. But he knew that he could not cross the barrier of the agents without having freed Habīb. The best thing he could do was to stay here and do his best to save Habīb and his friends.

In the morning, the boys had taken the herd out to graze. The white goat and Blacktail and the goats and the rest of the herd jumped up and down as they walked through the main alley of the village. Blacktail's friend was waiting for him at the end of the alley. Ali and Mālik did not have a lot of patience. All their attention was focused on Abdullah. They were wondering whether or not he had been able to do his job and was able to put all of the guards to sleep and free the four prisoners. They were occupied with these thoughts when the sound of a horse's hooves terrified the herd. Two riders passed quickly without paying any attention to the herd. The poor animals were terrified. Ali knew one of the riders. It was Amr, who was riding fast. He wondered if this meant that Abdullah had been able pull it off. Had they learned of the prisoners' escape? Is that why they were galloping so fast?

In the desert, Amr had pummeled and kicked Abdullah. He had beaten him on his back, head, and face with a whip.

"What did you do, you miserable wretch?" growled Amr.

"They are lying about me. I did not do anything!" whimpered Abdullah.

"I will show you what you did. You work for us, you eat our food, but you bark for others, you miserable dog!"

The shepherds were standing and watching what was happening. They were so frightened that they could not even intercede. Two of them, who were beggars in Kūfa, had escaped misery with Abdullah's help, and now had a family of their own. Abdullah cried out in pain, and begged Amr not to hit him each time Amr whipped and punched and kicked him. But his pleadings fell on deaf ears. Two or three others who were even more ruthless than Amr came to his aid. They beat Abdullah so badly that they left no healthy place on his body and bloodied his head and face.

Abdullah was made to suffer so much pain that he eventually lost consciousness. One of the shepherds had seen Abdullah pouring something into the guards' drinking water at night and quickly took the water over to them. Just to be on the safe side, the guards had told

Abdullah to drink some of the water himself first. This he had done, and it had put him into a deep sleep for several hours.

Abdullah was thrown into the tent where the prisoners were kept. Habīb was surprised to see him in such a condition. Salman crawled over to him. He brought his face in front of his big nose. His mouth was tied so he could not speak, but it was clear from his nodding that Abdullah was alive. He made some unintelligible sounds when he was being beaten, which Habīb and the others could not understand, which is why Habīb still looked at him with loathing.

Ali constantly wandered between the sheep, going back and forth. Mālik was sitting on the shore, this time telling the fish of his woes, rather than trying to catch them. His cheeks were wet with tears. From time to time, he turned his head to see how Ali was doing. The sun had not yet reached its zenith when they could no longer bear it and gathered the herd with difficulty and headed back to the village. The poor creatures did not want to return so soon.

The old men of the village were talking with each other and spreading some news. Amr's agents constantly went back and forth between the village and the encampment of the Kūfan army, and they had brought the news that Ibn Ziād would lift the siege of Husain ibn Ali's ؑ caravan and let him return to Medina only if the Imam pledged allegiance to Yazīd. That was what the whole affair boiled down to. On the other hand, Husain ibn Ali ﷺ refused to pledge allegiance to the head of a tyrannical government, who had built ostentatious palaces for himself and adorned mosques in the Levant with money stolen from the public purse. But what was even worse than that was that Yazīd, who was Muʿāwiya's son and successor, in contrast to Muʿāwiya himself, who at least maintained a semblance of abiding by the sacred law, openly violated it in public. Many had reported seeing him playing with a monkey whilst drunk.

These were the words that were being exchanged between the old men of the village, who at one time were the warriors of their tribe. Now everyone knew that there would be a bitter battle before too long – a fight to the death. Doubts and suspicions were on the rise. Maybe if these men were younger, they too would have wanted to join up with Imam Husain ﷺ as Habīb and his friends had tried to do; or perhaps, like Saʿd's father, they would have trampled on that which is right for the sake of worldly gains.

Umm Habīb had been sitting by the front door since early morning in order to obtain any news she could of what had taken place in the desert encampment. Ali and Mālik arrived, and when they saw Umm Habīb sitting at the door in the state that she was in, they realized that no news had reached her yet.

Amr and Saʿd were talking in the courtyard. Amr's eyes were red with anger.

"I am sure that it is the work of those rebellious boys." Said Amr.

"Ali is smarter than that. There is nothing he wouldn't do if he got it into his head to free his father." Replied Sa'd.

"Even begging you to free them?"

Amr gave Sa'd a meaningful look. Sa'd was standing still, staring at Amr. He had raised a big question: What would he do if Ali did beg him for mercy?

"Perhaps..."

"So be prepared for that eventuality. And tell your father not to fall for such a ploy."

"I cannot do that. I have barely been able to endure what has taken place already."

Amr put his hand on Sa'd's shoulder and said, "So you deserve to be treated like the helpless boy that you are."

Sa'd shook Amr's hand off his shoulder in disgust.

Amr went to his horse and took him by his reins. He shouted out to Sa'd who was walking towards the house, "If I were you, I would be going to Ali right now and telling him to forget about resisting the inevitable. Then you would see how he would be reduced to begging."

Habīb was sitting by Abdullah's head. He could not understand why they had beaten him up so badly. There were a few slices of bread and a couple of bowls of water and milk in the tray being held by a guard, who was looking at Habīb with apprehension. The guard said, "I brought you some food, but I'll only give it to you on the condition that you don't get me in trouble when I untie your mouth."

Habīb relieved the guard's concern with a nod of his head. The guard sat down and set the tray to one side and untied Habīb's hands and mouth, and then did the same for everyone else. There were several other guards keeping watch outside as well. As soon as Habīb's mouth had been untied, he asked about Abdullah, "Why did they treat him like this?"

The guard looked at Habīb and said quietly, "Because he tried to put us to sleep and help you escape."

Habīb was shocked. Why did he want to help them escape after having betrayed them?? And if he was not the one who had betrayed them, then who was? Salman went over to see to Abdullah before eating his bread and milk. He gently touched his face and sprinkled a few drops of water from the bowl on his face.

"Look at the state he has gotten himself into because of us. But you said that he was to blame for the trouble we are in," said Salman.

"I don't understand it. No one knew about our plans other than him and Umm Habīb." said Habīb.

Salman gently wiped Abdullah's face with a corner of his handkerchief. He gradually opened his eyes. His teeth were broken, and he had lost a lot of blood. Habīb came over and called him several times.

"Leave him alone and eat your food. I have to tie your hands and mouths again. Don't make any trouble for me," scowled the guard.

Habīb called out to Abdullah again. Abdullah spoke in a muffled voice, spitting out blood as he talked, "It was Sa'd. Sa'd and Ali and Mālik wanted to come with us. But Sa'd deceived the boys."

Habīb could no longer bear to look at Abdullah's face: the face of a boy who had foregone the only memento he had of his mother in order to be able to join Husain ibn Ali's ﷺ caravan, and who had then been accused of being a snitch. He placed his head on Abdullah's forehead and asked for his forgiveness.

———◆———

The sound of someone knocking on the front door broke the pervasive silence of the house. Ali and Mālik ran out. Umm Habīb stood behind the door and waited to see who was behind the door at this time of night. Everyone was waiting impatiently for news of what was going on; waiting for any news that would save them from their unbearable uncertainty.

Everyone was quiet for a moment when the door was opened. If Blacktail had not barked and taken Ali and Mālik out of their shocked state, they would not have been able to recognize the person standing behind the door. Sa'd was standing at the door, staring into Ali's eyes. His father's high hopes for him and his reprimands for his failure to achieve them had made an unpredictable creature out of Sa'd. Ali hesitated for a moment. His eyebrows furrowed and he was about to close the door on Sa'd, but Sa'd put his foot inside the door and prevented him from doing so.

"I have a message for you." said Sa'd.

Ali gave him a disapproving look. He wanted to pummel Sa'd right there with his hands and feet. He could not stand to hear his voice.

"The sleeping herbs did not work. Abdullah is now imprisoned with your father."

The news hit Ali like a pail of hot water being poured on his head. He suddenly felt very hot all over. He slammed the door so hard that if Sa'd had pulled his foot out a moment later, his foot would have been crushed between the door and its frame. Ali leaned against the door and began to sob. If Ali had not decided to follow his father; or even if it had only been him and Mālik who had known about his decision, he would not be in this situation he was now in. Umm Habīb and his mother and sisters were suffering here in the village, and his father and his friends were suffering out in the desert, all because of a decision for which he bore all the responsibility.

For his part, Sa'd just started at the door that had been slammed in his face, dumbfounded. He was expecting Ali to fall at his feet after hearing this news and beg him to do something to free his father.

8

Everything was in disarray. Ali's father was imprisoned. Husain ibn Ali's ﷺ caravan was arrayed against the Kūfan army. There was every possibility of war in the air. And Ali was alone. He could not reach the caravan, nor could he do anything to save his father. He did not want to dash Umm Habīb's pride. He knew that if Umm Habīb went to Sa'd's father and begged him for mercy, she would only be humiliating herself. What they were interested in was to take advantage of the standoff of this battle to garner some advantage for themselves, and there was no greater advantage that could be had than their arresting a few people who wanted to go to the aid of the Prophet's grandson against the wishes of the government and contrary to its official decree.

He thought of going and begging Sa'd to free his father and his friends, reminding him of the times of their friendship; but then he thought that Sa'd would humiliate him. Sa'd was someone who gave up his best friend in order to garner the praise and attention of his father, and so he was not someone who would agree to such a request. Their erstwhile friendship was meaningless to him. Mālik and Umm Habīb and the others had fallen asleep. But Ali kept walking around and around in the courtyard under the light of the stars.

Realizing that their noisemaking would not get them anywhere, Habīb and his friends had chosen not to make noise so that their mouths would be left untied. Abdullah had been somewhat rejuvenated with Salman's help. At night, everyone only ate their bread, leaving the milk for Abdullah. He was beaten up so badly that it would take a month of his being bedridden in order for him to recover.

"Everyone else was either killed by the Kūfan forces or was at least able to reach there. But we..." said Habīb, his voice quivering.

"Who knows what this bastard wants to do to us. And whose prison is this anyway, Ibn Ziād's or Amr's??" said Salman.

"You are lucky. Amr wanted to hand you over, but Ibn Ziād did not want you. Even now, everywhere is crawling with his men. No one can move a muscle." Said Abdullah under his breath, painfully taking short breaths.

"This lack of information is killing me. It is not clear what is going on out there!" said Salman.

Early in the morning, Mālik knocked on the wooden doors of the houses of the village one by one. When the doors opened, he said something and hurried to the next house, followed by Blacktail and his canine friend.

Umm Habīb was sitting in the courtyard, staring at the door. Ali and Samā and the others were standing around her. Ali said, "This is the only option we have left. If they don't accept it, we won't be able to do anything else."

"Just the fact that they had the courage to try to help the grandson of the Prophet is a great thing in and of itself. Do not worry, my boy; we are doing our best. God is on our side."

These words of Umm Habīb's were a great comfort to Ali, who constantly blamed himself for the situation. He had asked Umm Habīb to ask the men of the village to go to Sa'd's father and try to do something to free Habīb and his friends. The men entered the courtyard one by one. Their tall stature and large arms signaled that all the men of the tribe were brave warriors who were ready for battle.

Umm Habīb asked them either to go to battle against Amr and his agents to free the men of the tribe and to fight, or to go to Sa'd's father's house to intercede with him to obtain their freedom. Who knew what would happen to them if they remained imprisoned? Mālik and Ali waited to see the reaction of the men, but everything went against their expectations. The men apologized in turn and made their excuses, saying that they could not go up against Amr and his men, especially since he was now allied with Umar bin Saʻd and would imprison anyone who dared to make a move against the Umayyad rulers. They each said what they had to say, then took their leave. Maybe they were right. The fate of Habīb and his friends and Abdullah was not something that could be ignored easily.

It was all over. Ali's father was a prisoner now, and no one could leave the village. The dispute between the two sides had also reached a critical stage, and reports indicated that the Prophet's grandson was besieged by an army of several thousand men.

Ali was despondent and no longer held out any hope. This time he had lost to Saʻd. But it was not a loss that would be talked about for a while and then forgotten. This time he had lost the competition in such a way that the bitterness of defeat would remain in his mind for the rest of his life. Umm Habīb, who could not think of anything else to do, leaned against the door of her house and stared at the end of the alley. Maybe this time she really had gone crazy.

Ali had imprisoned himself inside the house. Mālik and his mother wanted him to take the herd out to pasture so that his thoughts would not bother him so much. He comforted himself with the fact that he was not guilty of any wrongdoing and did not know that Sa'd intended to betray him. He stayed at home until the evening. The call to prayer

came from the roofs of houses. Umm Habīb was still leaning against the door and would not go into the house. A man on horseback hurried through the village. Umm Habīb's eyes followed the man. She came into the house quickly and said with gusto, "My Habīb has come. He is on horseback."

Everyone was surprised. Ali shook his head. He thought that Umm Habīb had become delusional. Silence took over the house. Umm Habīb herself began to doubt whether she had really seen a rider or if she had imagined it. It didn't take long before there was a knock at the door. A boy knocked on all the houses and invited the people to gather in the main ally of the village.

It was not clear what had transpired. Ali and Mālik left the house with every other curious member of the family. Their neighbors were walking in the same direction too. The golden rays of the sun still illuminated the streets of the village. A large crowd had gathered in the main ally of the village.

Everyone was saying something. Ali went ahead to get a better idea of what the news was going to be.

"They say that he has been sent by the grandson of the Prophet."

"His countenance is awe-inspiring, like a true warrior!"

"He is a messenger of Husain ibn Ali's."

He had reached the village with difficulty. He asked the people to be calm with a movement of his hands. Someone from the crowd said in a loud voice, "Be calm, people. The gentleman's name is Habīb ibn Maẓāhir. He has brought you a message from Husain ibn Ali."

When the crowd heard this, everyone became silent. Everyone listened expectantly.

The old man started his speech by sending blessings unto the Prophet of Islam, and then said, "I call on you on the basis of the honor and greatness that will be yours on the Day of Judgment. The grandson of your prophet is surrounded in the desert of Karbalā; he is alone and is being treated unjustly. The people of Kūfa invited him to come to them, and now that he has come, they have abandoned him and are ready to fight him. I swear by God, if any of you are killed along with Husain, he will be a friend and companion of God in the highest positions in Paradise."

Habīb ibn Maẓāhir spoke loudly to the people and invited the warriors of the village to take up the sword to help Husain ibn Ali ﷺ and stand against the Kūfan army, which intended to murder him. At this time, the people, who had heard the words of the Prophet's grandson from the mouth of Habīb ibn Maẓāhir, had a change of heart. A man named Abdullah bin Bashar recited a poem that talked of the resurrection of courage. It was as if the people were no longer afraid of Amr and Saʿd's father and of their rulers.

> *Those who stay on the sidelines will know that the*
> *awe of the soldiers will be broken in battle.*
> *I am a warrior, a warrior of the battlefield, like a*
> *roaring lion with sharp claws.*

These poems delighted Ali. Perhaps Habīb ibn Maẓāhir's appearance was a gift from God to Ali and Umm Habīb, who wished that all the men of the village would think like they did. Habīb ibn Maẓāhir quickly got on his horse and passed through the darkness of the alleys and made his way back to the caravan. Ali wished he could have gone with him.

The men of the village had become emboldened by the speech. Everyone decided to sharpen their swords by nightfall and gather in the village's main alley and to leave from there. In the meantime, Ali asked some of the men of the village, now that they were singing war songs, to go to the desert first and release his father and his friends.

Two of Amr's men rushed to tell him the news. Amr became very upset. Sa'd's father had become very concerned as well. They could no longer stop the huge number of men in the village with the few people that they had. Amr turned to Sa'd and said, "You have to reach Umar bin Sa'd and give him the news!"

"Me? At this time of night??"

"Yes. Take the same route that we took before. Move fast! There's not a moment to lose!"

Sa'd did not know what to do. He had been tormented by his conscience throughout the whole episode. If he conveyed the news to Umar ibn Sa'd, Umar would have prevented the warriors of the village from joining up with Husain ibn Ali ﷺ; but if did not get news to Umar ibn Sa'd, some people might be able to join forces with the Imam. And if he did not go, he would no longer have any standing with his father and his family. This was the best opportunity for him to show his courage and superiority to everyone.

About twenty men from the village arrived at the camp with Ali and Mālik, both of whom also had swords in their hands. The only thing that could be seen next to the tents was the light of the campfires. Everywhere was covered in absolute darkness. Even the moon was absent and did not light the way for them.

Habīb and his friends were surprised to hear the sound of swords and of the battle dirges of the men of their tribe. They fell silent for a moment in order to hear the sounds more clearly. Meanwhile, Ali and Mālik came up to the tents.

"Father...?" said Ali.

Habīb had become overwrought by emotion. The light of the torch that Ali was holding in his hand showed Abdullah sleeping with his head on Salman's knee.

"What's going on? Who have you come with??"

Ali was so happy he could not contain himself. God had given them a miracle.

"We came with the men of the village. The Prophet's grandson asked the villagers to come to his aid."

"You mean they came to the village themselves??" exclaimed Salman.

Mālik, who was quickly untying everyone's hands together with Ali, answered Salman joyfully, "No, he sent Habīb ibn Muẓāhir as his envoy. The way he spoke made everyone realize how mistaken they had been."

As soon as Habīb's hands were untied, he stood up quickly and picked Abdullah up and placed him over his shoulder and back. Then he said, "First we have to take this boy to the village and leave him with Umm Habīb. By the way, how is Umm Habīb doing?"

Sa'd rode his black horse with a torch in his hand and was putting a distance between himself and the village at a rapid clip. There was a great commotion in his heart. The all-black horse sped through the desert and was gaining ground on the battlefield. Who knew what kind of new misfortune awaited the unfortunate villagers if he were to succeed in his mission?

Little by little, the main alley of the village started to be filled with the warriors of the village, who reached the appointed place one by one. Amr was watching them from the safety of the roof of one of the surrounding houses together with his warriors, who numbered less than ten. He did not trust Sa'd. He was afraid that he would give up on his task in the middle of the road and seek to make up for his betrayal of his friends. But he knew that none of his own men were capable of reaching Umar ibn Sa'd. If Sa'd were not to be overcome by his emotions, he would be the only person who would be sufficiently motivated by his desire for acceptance by his father to brave the absolute darkness of that night and to reach the position of the Kūfan army.

It did not take long for Sa'd to reach some hills from which he could easily see the encampments of both camps. Each tent had its own torch. On one side, there were a few torchlights, and on the other side was a sea of countless torchlights. The sky was full of stars big and small, and a waxing gibbous moon could now be seen above the horizon. But there was a commotion on the ground. Sa'd suddenly saw the light of the tents, which were being put out one by one. He thought that perhaps Husain ibn Ali ﷺ had surrendered and wanted to strike the tents. But if that was the case, he would have waited until morning. No caravan was going to start to move in the darkness of night.

Sa'd was still ambivalent. A call from within called on him to go back the way he had come and join forces with Ali and Mālik and make up for all of his treachery. But the thought of being in charge of all the trade caravans and the honor and respect that was going to be bestowed on him got the upper hand and decided him to continue on his mission. He was standing on top of a hill. He struggled with himself for a moment, but ultimately headed for the main tent in the large encampment.

Everyone was talking about there being a fierce battle ahead. The battle was due to begin in the morning. The soldiers had gathered in groups of threes and fours and had gathered around the campfires they had started, talking about the battle that was before them. They described the events of previous battles, exaggerating certain details. Sa'd passed by their tents on horseback and made his way to the main tent.

When he dismounted, he was taken to the main tent. There were a lot of soldiers guarding the tent. When Sa'd arrived there, he heard it reported that Husain ibn Ali ﷺ had extinguished the torches of his tents. Umar ibn Sa'd sent several people to go over there and bring news of what was going on.

Umar ibn Sa'd became very upset upon hearing what Sa'd had to say. He commanded Arzaq bin Hārith to be brought to his presence. Sa'd stood silently in a corner of the tent watching the happenings within it. After a few moments, a brawny man entered the tent. It was Arzaq bin Hārith. As soon as he saw him, Umar ibn Sa'd issued the necessary instructions, "Take four hundred people and follow this boy. The people of his village are sympathizers of Hussain ibn Ali."

Sa'd took the lead on horseback, followed by a cavalry of four hundred warriors. The sound of the horses' hooves broke the silence of the desert.

The village warriors were slowly making their way out of the village together with Habīb. Amr was anxious and had begun to lose hope of getting help from Umar ibn Sa'd.

"It's over... Everything is over!"

Ali and Mālik had now attained their dream. More than a hundred men marched like a small army, with swords in hand. Some were on horseback and others were on foot.

Amr and his men came after them on horseback. After a while, the two armies faced each other. Sa'd was their forerunner. Ali and Mālik stared in disbelief as they saw Sa'd on his black horse leading hundreds of cavalry troops to block their way. Arzaq gave a signal with his torch, and Habīb moved his torch in response for his side, and they both walked towards each other. Amr, who witnessed the incident from afar, applauded Sa'd with joy.

When Arzaq came close to Habīb, he withdrew his sword from its sheath, and said, "Where are you going with all these people?!"

"This is the question I have for you. Our village is nearby. What business do you have here in this desert?" retorted Habīb.

"We have been informed that you are sympathetic to Husain ibn Ali's cause. Now go right back to where you came from!"

"We have not come this far in order to return!"

"Do not be foolish. Not a single one of you will cross this line alive!"

Habīb looked at his people. They were able to hear the words that were exchanged in the darkness of the night and the silence that reigned over it. Looking at Habīb, everyone raised their swords in support.

"You are making a mistake. Like Husain ibn Ali, you are up against a much larger army."

"His people may be few compared to your numbers, but whatever they are, they are on the side of that which is right."

"So be prepared. If you want to pass, then come forward."

Upon hearing this, the warriors went forward. A fierce battle ensued. When several of their men were martyred, Salman asked them to retreat. Everyone realized that they had left it too late, and that if they had acted a few days earlier, they could have gotten there more easily. Ali and Mālik went to Habīb, who was lying down. He had taken several blows of the sword, but he was still alive. He turned his eyes to the road that led to the caravan of Husain ibn Ali ﷺ. He softly uttered his testimony of faith and closed his eyes. Ali and Mālik wept silently. Sa'd was standing at a distance, watching the scene. He was the main cause of these events. If he had not betrayed his friends, Habīb and his friends would now be among Husain ibn Ali's ﷺ army. Arzaq and his army stood against the people like an immutable wall and gave no thought to returning. Perhaps they were thanking God for having left the scene of the main battle that was to come. Tomorrow would be a difficult day in the Nineveh desert.

10

The promised day had arrived. Amr and Sa'd's father went to join and serve the Kūfan army in order to curry favor with the ruling Umayyad elite. Amr spoke of Sa'd's courage the night before, and how it prevented their plans from failing. Sa'd was accompanying them. Now he had everything he wanted, but his heart was restless. The moment of Habīb's martyrdom and Ali and Mālik's silent weeping kept playing repeatedly before his eyes. He wanted to hit his head against a wall.

A fierce battle broke out between the two sides that day. Sa'd stood away from the battlefield together with his father in one of the tents, waiting to receive the reward for their service from the spoils of the battle.

In the evening, when the war was over and the soldiers of the Kūfan army were happily going back and forth gathering their share of the booty, Sa'd also walked over to the battlefield. It was a horrible display of the gruesomeness of war. Heads and arms that had been cut off were scattered everywhere. There were bodies which had been trampled under the hoofs of the horses of cavalry who had trampled over them. A woman's earrings dripping with blood could be seen in the hands of a soldier. Women and children were running everywhere between the tent fires to escape the reach of enemy soldiers. It was dusk and the sun's rays had taken on the color of blood. Sa'd was overcome by his emotions. He could not keep his eyes open. Everywhere he turned, there were signs of a terrible and cruel war.

The village was mired in a heavy silence that night. Umm Habīb had placed the boys' heads on her knees and was content knowing that Habīb had finally been martyred defending the Prophet's grandson's cause. Abdullah was limping along. Umm Habīb told the boys that now they were the men of the household and had to act like grown men. Everyone knew what had happened to the family of the Prophet that day in the desert of Ninawa. The thought of several thousand soldiers standing in front of a small caravan of 100 people who wanted nothing more than to be allowed to leave and go back to their homes, and then massacring them in cold blood, shocked everyone to the very core of their being.

All the men of the village had gathered in one place. They wanted to leave early in the morning. Arzaq and his cavalry had left. It was a difficult night. No one could sleep.

Early in the morning, when the sun slowly rose from the vast expanse of space, Ali and Mālik went to the desert of Nineveh together with a large number of men from the village. A great sorrow weighed heavily on their chests.

When they reached the plain of Karbalā, the tents of the Kūfan army had already been struck. The army had departed before the villagers arrived. The smell of blood was everywhere. The heads of the martyrs were gone, taken as souvenirs and mementos by the victors. The burnt remnants of tents could be seen smoldering in the morning light. All that was left were headless bodies that had been crushed and otherwise violated. It was as if one was witnessing a scene from the Day of Resurrection.

Ali looked at the sky and whispered a promise to his recently martyred father. "Father, I promise you I will never forget these scenes. I will tell the story to everyone, and make sure that everyone understands the significance of your sacrifice and the lengths you went to in doing that which is right and in order to ensure that justice prevails."

The villagers started to prepare the bodies of the martyrs for burial.